I0610742

Falling into Congo

Fighting Off the Poachers

Stan Bindell

Contact Stan

thebluesmagician@gmail.com

Published by: Writers Publishing House
Printed in the United States

ISBN: 978-1-64873-544-8

Contents

Foreword…. i

1

Green…. 1

2

White Rhin….17

3

Cynthia Baxter…36

4

PoRue Kazzie…. 71

5

Kyle Tsinnie…. 84

6

Massimo Ferrara…102

7

Lizzy Feinstein…. 114

8

Meeting in Africa….128

9

Adventure in Emeralds….153

10

Endangered Species….175

11

Politics, War and Peace…. 209

12

Golden Cat and Invasion…. 219

13

Coming Home….243

Author's Note….269

About the Author….271

Foreword

Ya'at'eeh shik'ee doo shidine'e!
('Hello to all my relations!')

The Navajo people and tribal peoples of the world have worked hard to retain their cultural bonds with the land for thousands of years. These trees of knowledge teach us all the means to live in concert and balance within the natural systems that all living beings call home.

These systems — our traditions — ensure that children are taught the value of the drum song, the heartbeat of the earth, the importance of elders and communal responsibility; to not take more than you need, to keep many things sacred without question or doubt, to ensure that animals are respected, even (and especially) when they become food; and to ensure that all offspring, neighbors and community know these teachings well, so that all will succeed in the endeavor of life.

The Navajos have a saying that embodies the idea of living in balance with all living things: '*Hozho.*'

I have learned through the years that this heartfelt sacredness is inherently human and shared by all. Every one of us at one time sang an Earthsong, drummed and felt the soul and spirit and pulse of Mother Earth, and knew all the natural laws and teachings that ensure our common path.

This book is written to inspire and reignite the fire that burns within all of each of us to do what is right, and learn from the teachings of tribal peoples who continue to hold steadfast to time-honored systems of knowledge, including those of the Navajo of the American desert Southwest.

In my friend Stan Bindell's wonderful book *Falling into Congo,* Sky, a young Native American man, finds himself lost, as so many of us do at some point in our lives. At once we are captivated through the eyes of Sky, who is inspired to find himself once again through the shared experience of other peoples — in this case, those who live in the heart of Africa — who fight every day to save what is sacred.

One of the other key figures is Kyle, who is Navajo and lives by Navajo values. These include Navajo songs, prayers and dances, as well as listening to the tribal elders, the language and teachings about community and harmonious life, the care for plants and animals, and most importantly, ensuring that kids know the tools for a successful balanced life — all of which continues still, under the relentless onslaught of modernization and constant pressure to acculturate. Warriors such as Sky and Kyle continue to work to protect what is sacred.

My hope for you is that as you read this book, you also listen to that inner voice and think about what is important.

I hope it inspires you to make a difference. The future of our planet and human populations are tenuous. Climate change most likely will be devastating to all, especially to our tribal communities. The wanton and prodigious ongoing slaughter of endangered species continues to be a lifetime battle for frontline warriors.

In the face of such manifold, overwhelming challenges, the teachings of Kyle's Navajo people — and other First Nations tribal peoples of the world, those who still know the way and teachings — become paramount. They are the repositories and source of unique knowledge to ensure our future survival.

So read and reflect, and listen to that inner song, that tells the tale of you and all you've come to know and love, and how connected we are on this shared, rare earth; and think too of what the book ignites in you.

Ahxehee! ('Thank you!')

Tony Skrelunas

Tony is a member of the Navajo Nation, raised within the cultural teaching systems by his great grandparents. He works to preserve what is sacred, extending to tribal knowledge systems to ensure our future survival. He works to preserve our tribal ways, including traditional food systems, respectful economies, and ensuring that Native peoples across the planet communicate in these challenging times. His unique outlook is best captured on website: www.valleyleadership.org/tony-skrelunas-interview

1

Green

All he could see was green. This wasn't just any green, either; it was the deepest, lushest, most vibrant green he had ever seen, anywhere. Well, as far as he could remember. That was funny, because just then he realized he couldn't remember much — in fact he couldn't remember anything at all.

He didn't know where he was, and even more, didn't have a clue about where he'd come from, nothing. It was all one big blank space in his head. A void.

Most troubling of all, he didn't even know who he was. He couldn't think of his name.

But: *look at that green!* Up and down, right and left, he was enveloped, surrounded by green. His eyes began to focus, and the green became blotches, the blotches slowly started turning into leaves ....

None of this made sense.

To his sudden horror, he saw he was naked. *Naked! Why?* That too made no sense. *Naked is for showers, baths, and for … for putting on clothes, but … where is here, anyway?*

Wherever this was, it had to be the most beautiful place on earth. Make that the most beautiful *green* place on earth. He gazed in wonder.

Strange birds made peculiar calls in the trees around him, trees so tall and thick he couldn't see the sky. He wondered how close he was to civilization.

Self-consciously he picked a leaf, which was huge, perhaps a foot long. The leaf had sticky sap, which he used to make a sort of loincloth for both front and back.

He began to walk, aimlessly, and wondered what he could find besides trees. He had to bend the plants and branches to pass. This was going to take a while. He picked up a long stick and used it to chop at and push the vegetation away. The humidity was horrible.

Even in his makeshift leaf loincloth, he was drenched in sweat.

Unable to see the sky, he wondered if it was day or night; not knowing was a little scary. He wished he had a watch. As he cut his way through the jungle, he started counting to a thousand to keep his mind occupied and see how far he could get while counting that high.

Before long he was hungry — really hungry. He didn't know where or how to get food. He didn't know where he would sleep. He hadn't a clue about how to survive, or even if he would. *Yikes.*

What's more, he didn't know if he was heading toward anything at all, apart from death. He counted to one thousand five times. At last, he sat to rest, not sure if there were a reason to carry on. He mopped his brow with the back of his wrist.

The screeches of animals and birds were getting louder. They were scary, but somehow a comfort, too. They helped him feel not so alone. Now, though, it was getting hotter, and he would soon need water. *Get up.* Again, he flailed at the tangled underbrush with his stick.

This went on for hours. Over and over, he would count to a thousand and begin again. Eventually he gave up counting and simply rested when too tired to continue on.

Reaching the point of complete exhaustion, he doubted he would survive. More precisely, he couldn't think of a reason why he *wouldn't* die. The inevitability of his imminent demise overwhelmed him, not merely because that would mean the end, but because he could not, for the life of him, remember whether he had a family, wife, lover, or any friends to mourn him.

Getting up, ready to use his machete-stick again, he heard a new sound. It sounded like … *water,* coming from the direction he'd been moving. He was thirsty. His mouth was dry. *Pray this isn't a hallucination ....*

He frantically hacked and banged his way forward. He chopped and chopped, then chopped some more. It seemed like forever.

Nearly ready to give up, at last he found a stream, clear, cold and fresh.

He dropped to his knees and dunked his head, then his body to his shoulders in the sparkling water, not caring about anything else. He cupped his hands and drank his fill. He caught his breath, laughed, and drank some more. He scooted to the edge and dangled his feet and legs in the chilly stream. Then he laid back, enjoying the slash of blue sky above. He was filled with hope.

He decided to follow it downstream, hoping it might lead to some type of civilization. In the trees, strange birds of every color impatiently waited for him to pass so they could take their turn at the water.

He continued his slog for what seemed an eternity. Then he paused, half believing he heard drums; but the sound was faint. *Could have imagined it.*

The pounding grew louder — so much so that he couldn't deny it, they were drums. The rhythm originated in a hard-packed clearing beyond a tangle of undergrowth that now blocked his path.

Fearing for his life, he dropped to the ground and bellied up to a slit in the growth. Trembling, he carefully raised his head, peering over a ridge of moss-covered rocks into a bright, broad meadow.

He nearly gasped — just feet away, a group of strangely decorated men, their bodies smooth and dark, drummed and frantically danced. Their faces were gruesome with paint, and hard, sculpted, glistening limbs moved to the pounding beat.

Suddenly a voice behind. *"Salut, ami. Avez-vous perdu quelque chose dans la brousse?"* ('Hey, friend. Did you lose something in the bush?')

He jumped, backpedaling into the verdant stone ridge. Three tall men with chiseled faces peered at him. Each carried a spear, and one had a long, narrow rawhide shield painted with a symbol reminiscent of the sun.

"Uh, uh, w-what? H-hello?" he stammered.

The three looked from one to the other.

"Parles-tu Français?" asked the largest. His smile was disarming.

He struggled to his feet, dumbly asking, "What? Uh, hello?"

The three laughed. "Ah, English," said the tall one. "He speaks *la* English. *Merveilleux!* We too speak the English words. We learned them at the *missionnaire. Très bon.* I speak *la* English, *très bon,* like a professional!"

He continued grinning ear to ear and offered the frightened stranger a steadying hand. "Are you British? American? Maybe a Canadian, eh?"

Still overwhelmed, he managed a response. "Uh ... uh, not sure ... um, where are we, anyway?"

The man patted him on the shoulder, and with a friendly laugh, said to his companions, "American! He's lost; he must be an American."

"I think I'm American," he answered at last. "I don't remember. I need some food — a-and clothes."

"We can arrange that, but what's your mission here?" the man asked.

"Mission ... mission ... uh, I'm just *here*," he said.

"You're bloody visiting. You certainly have an odd way of dropping in. Ahh, *you* were the one who dropped from the sky, weren't you?" the tall man asked.

"Dropped in? What do you mean?"

"Somebody dropped in from the sky, came down on a parachute. There aren't many visitors here, or ways to get here, so I think that was you."

The visitor shook his head, not knowing what to tell them. Not knowing what they would accept. Not knowing what they would believe.

The spokesman saw perplexity in the visitor's face. "Okay," he said, "let's give you something to eat. Maybe you can get your bearings and we can sort this out."

The tall man pointed to the trail leading down to their camp, gesturing to follow.

The visitor looked around, still baffled as to where he was. He couldn't get over the size of the plants: they were taller and thicker than any he'd ever seen — and maybe like nothing he would see again.

Back to reality. What was he to tell his hosts?

"You speak English, but you said you also speak French?" he asked, starting to feel comfortable among the three who had startled him.

"The French came years ago and sent us to boarding schools, where we were forced to learn French and then English rather than our own language," he explained as they walked.

Before long they came to a village filled with colorful huts: orange, red, green, purple, blue, yellow; almost every hue imaginable. No two of any one color ever sat side by side.

These were rondavels, round huts made from local materials, usually sand, soil and sometimes cow dung. This tribe used bamboo instead, from the nearby river. Bamboo is also easier to paint than the other available materials.

Hundreds of villagers started to appear from their colorful rondavels.

Some were curious to see the visitor. Men went about their business. Women and children watched with a curious eye. All of the villagers were Black. The visitor noticed he wasn't quite the same color.

He blurted out, "Where am I?"

"Don't you know?" His trail guide responded. "I guess you're telling the truth. You really *don't* know where you are, my friend. Welcome to Congo. You are in the heart of Africa."

***

The trail guide introduced himself. "I'm Joseph. What's your name?"

He scratched his head.

"I … I … come to think of it, I don't know my name."

"Ah. Now we're getting somewhere. That explains a lot. You must have some sort of amnesia. Hopefully it will come back. Until it does, we have to call you something. I think we'll call you Sky."

"I can live with that," said Sky.

"You can stay here as long as you want. Do you have somewhere to go?" Joseph asked.

"None that I know of," Sky said. "So … where will I stay?"

"We will show you a rondavel. You will have it to yourself. We're hours from any city, and transportation isn't cheap, so we sustain ourselves. Do you hunt, or fish?"

"Not sure. I might."

Joseph nodded.

A few of the people showed him the way to his designated lodging. He went inside as one of the men watched. He found a cot with blankets, a dresser and a light. He seemed surprised.

The men laughed.

"We have light. We need it for reading, you know."

"But where does the electricity come from?"

"We have solar. An American company came over a year ago and set up their panels. It changed our way of life."

Joseph, who had kept him company, elaborated.

"It is better for us than it used to be, and we are far away from Congo's troubles: the politics, murders, rapes, torture, the poaching of some of the most beautiful animals in the world in some of the most beautiful places in the world. What do you think of that, Sky?"

Sky didn't know.

"We're frustrated. I love my Congo. I love my people, but, what do we do? How long before it comes to us, here in our tiny village?"

"I wish I could help," Sky said.

Joseph peered at him.

"How old are you?

Sky looked perplexed.

"I don't remember that either."

"I think you're seventeen or eighteen."

"How do you figure?"

"We're good at gauging a person's age because we have manhood ceremonies when he turns thirteen, and add to his manhood feathers each year until he reaches eighteen. The teens earn them by providing food for their families, whether by hunting or working the fields to raise crops. Based on your size and facial features, I'm estimating your age.

"I'm also basing my guess on your maturity. If you were younger and couldn't remember your own name or how you got here, you would be freaking out. You're handling this well, considering your condition. So, all in all, that tells me you can't be much older than eighteen."

"It'll be good to know, along with all the other things I can't remember," Sky said.

Another man extended his hand.

"My people call me Heart. Maybe I can help you figure this out in the morning," he offered.

"How did you get the name Heart?" Sky asked.

"Because they say I wear my heart on my sleeve. Can't you see?" He hesitated, then laughed.

"Maybe I'll remember things in the morning." *I hope.*

***

The sun beamed into the rondavel in faint shafts of morning light. Sky looked outside and saw a bright orange sun, brighter than any he could recall; yet that thought brought cold comfort, since he couldn't recall much of anything at all.

Just outside the hut, people were milling around; children played, women were laughing. No men in sight, but this seemed a happy place. Heart appeared from around the corner wearing his big smile.

"We greet the sun for you," he said to Sky warmly. "Get what you need and come with me. It's time for breakfast."

Sky quickly dressed and followed Heart.

At breakfast, Sky saw Joseph among hundreds of people sitting around tables, waiting for him. Rising, Joseph reached out his hand to shake.

"Good morning! Sit down in friendship. I want to chat with you. Are you okay this morning? Do you know who you are?" Joseph asked.

Sky scratched his head and laughed.

"I feel good. I feel healthy, but no, I still don't remember anything. Not even my name."

"Nothing at all, eh?" Heart asked.

"Nothing at all. My memory seems blank."

Joseph looked him over, head to toe.

"Do you remember the difference between right and wrong?" Joseph asked.

"I sure hope so," Sky responded.

"Well, can you give me an example of right and wrong?"

"I'll take it backward." Sky thought. "Wrong is when somebody rapes, steals and kills. Right is when somebody prevents any of those crimes."

Joseph smiled. "That's a great answer. Some might find your answer extreme, but in the jungle, many of those atrocities go on. Here in our little village, though, we have none of that. It's only when we have to protect our village that we do what we have to — self-defense and all that. Most who are corrupt and vicious don't know we're here. They don't want to come this far into the bush. So, our people know that if they stray too far, they are vulnerable. Here we have what we need."

Sky listened, intent.

Joseph had more to say. "We have our concerns about those who are corrupt. Although still far from us, they are creeping closer; at some point we will have to do something different.

"Our village is concerned about all living things. The plants, the animals, the wildlife, the frogs. One of our special animals is the white rhinoceros. In our religion we have a unique relationship with that animal. If the white rhinoceros disappears, many believe that *we* disappear — and the numbers are decreasing due to poachers. The bastards kill the white rhinos to sell their horns to those who especially want them and then sell the meat as well. It's like taking our soul when they take our white rhinoceros."

Sky said he never heard anything like that before. "You have a different type of life here, apart from anything I've heard or dreamed; but I am concerned about the environment and endangered species. What can we do to stop the poachers?"

Joseph liked the sound of *we*; he said they patrol the area as much as they can. "We set off warning shots if any of the poachers are getting close," he explained. "They usually think that no one is here to stop them, so even though they are armed, when they hear guns shooting in their direction, usually they run off. We know they go to other places to poach the rhinos or other large game animals, but we can only be concerned about protecting our village, our people, our animals. Our resources are limited."

"Can I see them?" Sky asked.

"The white rhinos?"

"Yes, they sound cool."

"That's a good idea." Joseph considered. "Our poaching-prevention team leaves in a couple hours. I'll go with you. We'll get you some boots and camouflage clothes."

"Camouflage?"

"Yes, we like to sneak up on poachers. They also use camo. It's as though we're both hiding from each other and looking for each other," Joseph mused.

"So, in the middle of nowhere, where do you get your clothes and hiking boots?" Sky asked.

"Ah, from the IPA," Heart chimed in.

"I thought the IPA was a kind of ale?"

Joseph laughed.

"Of all the things that you could remember, you remember that!

"Not India Pale Ale," Joseph continued. "Our IPA is the International Poaching Association. It should actually be the International Poaching Prevention Association, but I guess they liked the shorter name. Anyway, it's a great organization that does what it can to support those who do whatever they can to prevent poaching."

"What do you do when you catch the poachers?"

"We kill them." Joseph laughed. "Kidding. We keep them here and we pay them better than do the greedy poachers to work on our team *against* poaching. Most of them like us a lot, and the better pay helps them live better. They also feel better about themselves when they join us. But the ones we cannot change, well, we ship them off to prisons in faraway places so they cannot come back."

Joseph explained that when they go to see the rhinos, they'll have to drive a few miles, then park their jeeps and hike in, so as not to startle them.

"Nobody wants an angry white rhino," he cautioned.

Sky asked again why poachers must kill the rhinos, as he could not see any logic to it.

"Mostly for the money, because of the horns," he explained. "The Chinese and some others believe that the horns will help them spiritually or give them sexual powers. Some also use the horns for jewelry. If the horns are cut off right, they will grow back; but the poachers are so lazy they usually just kill the rhinos. Sometimes they try and drug them, but the drugs are too strong and often kill them. It's a shame. Many fear the white rhino because it is so large, but unless provoked he is a peaceful animal. The ones that survive horn-cutting need help. Without their horns, they can't survive as well in the wild, so we take them in. After a while, they become so tame that we can hand-feed them."

Sky asked if the white rhino is the only animal they care about.

"Oh, no," said Joseph. "Our people believe in protecting all living beings except for what we hunt to eat. But the white rhino is among the special creatures that we never hunt or eat. The white rhino is the most special of all species to us."

Joseph told Sky to finish his breakfast and get dressed.

"You're about to learn about our special creature," he said.

2

White Rhino

Within minutes, twenty or so jeeps drove up with the tribesmen in camouflage. All were armed with handguns, semiautomatic rifles and a range of equipment, ready to go into the bush. Joseph jumped out of the third vehicle, approached Sky, and again shook his hand.

"You may not know who you are, but I'm convinced you're a good man. We trust you to go with us. We trust you to join us, not only physically but in spirit. If you were to betray us, many of us would die and we could lose our way of life. The madmen who back the poachers will kill us if they get the chance. We cost them millions when we protect the white rhino and they can't get the horns to sell on the black market. That is their way of life. We believe it is not a good way of life. Indeed, we want to keep the white rhino alive — not only for its life, but to preserve our ways, our country and our environment. When people have a way of life, they will do anything to protect it."

Sky responded by saying he respected their way of life, especially their work to protect the white rhino. Then, excited, he jumped in with Joseph and the jeep sped off into the haze of an African morning sun. Heart was in the jeep right behind.

As they zipped through the forest, Sky was once again mesmerized by all the plush greenery. The farther the jeeps went into the woods, the more monkeys appeared in the trees. They shrieked at the jeeps and their noise became overwhelming.

From the surrounding woodlands, despite his failed memory, Sky could remember that this was the way the African savanna looked on television. When they started into the woods there were many trees, a somewhat dense forest; but as they approached their destination, the trees were more scattered among grassland.

So beautiful. Sky felt he could look at this and all it held forever.

Joseph could see Sky's face come alive.

"Yes, it is beautiful …," then added, "but it's the creatures that live in it that make it even better."

As they drove, they passed more and more wildlife: a herd of elephants as well as giraffes, hippopotamuses, lions, and grazing zebras that slowly made their way along, munching on the grassland. Gazelles were playing. They also saw a variety of antelope, including the roan and the bushbuck antelope. Even a few buffalo were seen on this range.

The trees were lit with bright colors from more than 300 bird species. The most eye-catching were the carmine bee-eaters, which come in bright red. The cattle egrets were not as colorful, but their plain white stood out against the green of the jungle.

"You see what I mean about our many creatures? We talk about the white rhino because it is the most endangered, but we love all our creatures. We have unique species of giraffes and elephants. We are one of the few places on earth where you can find both the African forest elephant and the African bush elephant. We have other animals that may be common, but they are part of us all the same," Joseph said. "We even love the spotted hyena."

After about an hour of driving through the woods, the jeeps started to slow, then crawled along before stopping.

Joseph jumped out. "Welcome to Garamba National Park. There may be no signs, but as soon as you see the beauty, you know you're here."

Joseph directed Sky to some nearby bushes.

"Look for movement in the bushes," Joseph said. "But be careful before taking action, as it could be anything. The poachers wear camouflage, we wear camouflage, and both sides stake out our claims in the bush. But the animals also move through the bush, so be careful not to act until you need to do so. Seconds can make a difference between life and death, so act quickly when you need to. We don't want to hurt the animals. Hopefully, you don't want to hurt us. Yet the poachers will kill or do whatever they feel they have to do to make their bounty. We take them alive when we can, but that isn't always the case."

Sky said he felt he was with the good guys. "You make everything so dramatic, so life and death."

"What would you do to protect your way of life?" Joseph asked.

Sky shook his head.

"I'm not sure, since I don't remember much, so I don't know what my way of life is," he replied.

"That is sad," Joseph countered. "We have our problems as a people, but we know who we are. Now it's time to move on, the white rhinos are just on the other side of the hill. We're going to walk quietly to the top so we can observe them. We have to approach slowly because we don't want to spook them. You don't want to see mad rhinos. They can be very deadly."

The anti-poaching regiment carefully made its way to the top of the hill. When they reached the crest, they looked out on fifteen white rhinos. Joseph passed his binoculars to Sky.

"They are *huge*," Sky marveled. "Beautiful, but huge. They seem docile."

Joseph replied that white rhinos are usually docile — but again, if spooked or in fear for their lives, they respond like any creatures who must defend themselves or their babies to survive.

The brigade stood watching for what seemed the longest time, but nobody appeared to notice, so involved were they in watching these enormous, carefree beasts.

"I know the large head stands out," Joseph said. "But check out the short neck and broad chest ... now, listen ...."

Sky listened intently, and sure enough, the rhinos were making a host of different sounds, including panting, grunting, snorting, squealing and bellowing. It was an odd and unexpected mix that emanated from these large mammals.

Still, their size was overwhelming: the head and body length reached up to thirteen feet, while the tail added more than two feet.

Sky momentarily looked away from the rhinos and into the distance, where he spotted a large body of water.

"What is that?" he asked Joseph.

"That's where Congo River and the Nile meet," Joseph responded. "The stream where you found the water is a tributary of Congo. The river is kind to us because it has created many marshlands, not only bringing us water, but the animals that like the water as well. The springs and marshes bring more plants. More plants bring elephants and other vegetarians."

Joseph said some of the problems caused by the poachers were the sound of the guns and the blood left after the kill. Both impact the rhinos left behind. After they come upon the dead or the bloody, they tend to stay as far away as possible from humans. As with other animals, rhinos have feelings and are less likely to breed after going through the trauma of hearing or seeing poaching.

"One can tell when the rhinos are upset," Joseph continued. "The horns will dip down to the ground. The heads will also look sullen."

The rhinos moved about, slowly eating the grass.

"You said this is a national park. Where are the park rangers?" Sky asked.

Joseph said most of the park rangers were scared off years ago by the poachers and their weapons. He said poachers would steal any equipment they could find in the park. So, the park eventually ran out of funds.

"They couldn't even maintain the park vehicles," Joseph said. "If they went out in the bush, they would return to find their homes had been vandalized and their food stolen. Soon the roads became impassable. It just became too much for most of them."

Sky noticed some of the bushes moving.

Joseph noted that sometimes it's just the wind. Soon the bushes stopped moving.

***

"I guess it's not the wind."

Joseph watched as his men lit out after the poachers in the bushes, who ran as soon as they saw the anti-poaching battalion.

The race was on. It took about three miles, but Joseph's unit caught up with them. The poachers didn't fire because they knew they were outnumbered and wouldn't survive. They surrendered. The anti-poachers sat them down and questioned them. When satisfied that no other poachers were in the area, they stayed around watching for a bit. As the day wore on, they decided to head back to camp with their prisoners in tow.

"Don't worry," Joseph assured Sky. "We are not like the poachers. We will treat them kindly. We will feed them and clothe them. We will talk to them about the problem with their ways and the problems they wreak on our society. We will also talk to them about improving their lives by working to save the white rhinos and other endangered species rather than poaching them for less money than we will pay them for preserving these wonderful creatures."

***

"All right," Joseph announced. "There is one more person I should tell you about. Nobody knows his name, but they call him the Black Robin Hood."

"Why?" Sky asked. "Who's Robin Hood?"

"He's a fictional character who steals from the rich to give to the poor. This Black Robin Hood lives in the forest and he protects the poor: only *these* poor are the white rhinos. And those who have seen a glimpse of him say he's Black. White rhinos, although big and mighty, are no match for poachers with guns and machetes. The Black Robin Hood appears out of nowhere and disposes of the poachers. There could be ten or more and only one of him, but he has no problem eliminating the outlaws. He is the mystery of this land because nobody knows where he came from or where he stays. He leaves nothing for trackers to follow.

"Unlike the real Robin Hood, he has no merry men. He acts alone. The problem is that this Robin Hood is not as kind as we are. He is but one man, so he has no place to put prisoners. He usually kills the poachers so they can't poach again. Sometimes he just leaves the bodies to let nature take its course. We don't like what he does. He gives us a bad reputation. Many don't believe that Black Robin Hood exists and that we are the ones who commit the violence, but Black Robin Hood is a fight we don't want.

"We have our hands full with the poachers, the drug runners and those who might encroach on our land and our way of life. We are doing our best to retain our ways. We don't need any more enemies, particularly one as cunning as Black Robin Hood. We have watched him work. We are sure he watches us as well. He has never hurt us or our people; sometimes when our people are in danger, he finds a way to help them. The law of the land says he is our ally, but he has a strange way of showing it. Enough said. It's time to head back to camp."

As they started the drive back, Sky asked what Joseph's people were called.

"Our proud people are the Wantu. Some get us confused with the Cantu, but those are Pygmies. You can see we are not Pygmies. The Cantu live down Congo River," Joseph said. "I like to talk about our proud Wantu people. We have evolved further than most societies — not in the sense of technology, but rather equality. Among our people, each treats the other well. There is no domestic violence. There is no infidelity. There is no cheating one another for personal gain.

"Our society is based on love and respect. Many societies preach that as a goal, but they don't live it. We do. We have found our own heaven on earth, but it's fragile. Fragile because there are other societies that would destroy us if they knew about us. They would destroy us for the sake of poaching. They would destroy us for the emerald and diamond mines. They would destroy us for our timber. Many societies or people in those societies make money their number-one goal. When money is number one in a society, character and all the other virtues come in a distant second or not at all. They cease to be goals their people strive to reach."

Joseph added that one other asset the Wantu have going for them is their health. "The medicine men in our tribe have found herbs in the forest and know what herbs to use for various diseases. Our people are unusually healthy. We are also lucky because many parts of Africa, even many parts of Congo, were colonized at one time or another, but our location is too remote; most of the land barons, mining companies, oil companies, timber companies and dictators have not come into this part of the jungle."

Joseph asked Sky if he wanted to remember everything he had forgotten. "Of course I do. Why would you ask that?"

"Because some people have something or many things in their past that they want to forget," Joseph guessed.

Sky said he didn't think of it that way. "I'm just thinking it would be nice to know who I am, where I'm from, whether I have a family, and what the heck I'm doing here."

Joseph laughed. "I've told you we are a healthy people because of our knowledge of the earth; our herbs. Well, we also have herbs for healing the memory. Tomorrow, we will go in search of those herbs, because we too would like to know who you are," Joseph said.

The jeeps pulled into the village to the sound of drums. Joseph said everyone should just have fun tonight with food and dance, because tomorrow they would go into the bush.

The drums grew louder and louder. Sky watched the villagers dancing: it looked improvisational, yet all were dancing in unison. Arms were stretched out with bodies straight and firm. The villagers clapped their hands to the beat, sometimes fast, sometimes in slow motion and at times in jerky rhythms that seemed to mock other types of dancers.

"We have two types of dances," Joseph explained. "We have social dances and ritual dances. Tonight, these are social dances. Nothing extremely happy to celebrate, like a wedding or coming of age or an upcoming harvest; but also nothing sad to dance about, like a funeral or a pending war. Sometimes our ritual dances get spiritual and really emotional."

Joseph continued to talk about the most popular dances of his tribe.

"Another dance that we get into is the *soukous*. It's kind of like a rumba," he said. "Sometimes we mix rock music into it, and then it's known as a *soukous ndombolo*. The rock version also involves a lot of gyrating. Some find it sexy; some find it obscene. In some parts of Africa this dance has been banned, but that just made it more popular."

Sky responded that something about the dances seemed familiar, but his memory failed him again.

Joseph said the *soukous ndombolo* has a lot of singing in it.

"But that's not surprising. Our people love to sing; our people are always singing. If they are happy, they sing. If they are sad, they sing. When they are working in the fields, they sing. They sing when they pray. They sing to the animals and to all of the Great Creator's beings. They sing to their children. They sing to their grandparents. I can hardly think of any situation where our people don't sing. You could say that we live in perfect harmony, but you will learn this and much more about our people the longer you stay with us," Joseph promised.

Sky listened intently, as he knew he was fast being accepted and valued in this foreign place. He remained deeply perplexed about not knowing who he was or where he was from, yet he knew he had landed in a good place and that life could be very much worse.

Joseph smiled and invited Sky to join him in a meal because they would need sustenance for the following day. Sky noticed that all the meals in the village were communal, that the people always ate together — and that they loved it, and wouldn't have it any other way.

As the women delivered the plates, Joseph explained that his people always feed the children first before the adults join in. Sky looked at his plate of brownish-gray food, not knowing what it was or what it would taste like.

Joseph burst out laughing.

"It's peanut soup! We have plenty of peanuts in the jungle and our people make the peanut soup. Very healthy."

Sky hesitated, but at last got up the nerve and took a spoonful.

"It's pretty good ... well, it tastes like peanuts, yet lighter than peanut butter and not as sticky," he admitted.

As they finished the peanut soup, the women brought out the next round. It was a stew with plenty of meat and vegetables, with yams and bread on the side. The fermented bread was called *kwanga,* made from cassava. Another side dish, looking a little like mashed potatoes, was delivered. Sky examined it as though trying to unravel a mystery.

Joseph could read Sky's face. "This is called *fufu.* It's made from yams, bananas and peanut butter. Again, like all our food, it's quite healthy," Joseph assured him. "We often roll it up into a ball and dip it into the soup. Quite tasty."

For dessert, the women brought some finger food. It was the kind that might look appealing with toothpicks for easy handling.

Sky eyed them skeptically. Even though the main meal passed the taste test, he wondered about this food.

Joseph smiled. "You should taste it before I tell you what it is," he suggested.

Sky confessed that while the food looked tasty, he was uneasy not knowing what it was.

Joseph took one more shot at persuading his guest. "You'll like it much better if you eat it before I tell you."

"I think I'll pass."

Seeing his prospects fade, Joseph gave in. "Okay. It's grasshoppers and caterpillars. I know, I know, but it sounds far worse than it tastes." He took a bite, as if to prove his point. "It has a nutty flavor. It's a good dessert and it has protein."

Sky made a face.

"Enough said. We leave in the morning for another adventure with the white rhinos."

***

Morning couldn't come soon enough. Sky felt excited about getting into the bush and learning more about this endangered species. The sun crept through his window, and the new day was here.

He dressed as quickly as possible. He ran out to eat a communal breakfast, then back to his room to gather up what he needed. *Good to go.* He looked outside. Joseph was standing ready with his usual big smile.

"All set."

"I thought that you might be," Joseph said. "So, let's go."

Five jeeps eased their way out of the camp, moving slowly, as usual, along the bumpy roads. The lush greens today were even more spectacular, with plenty of chittering monkeys and noisy colorful birds. After a couple hours' drive, they began to hear guns in the distance.

"That's not a good sign." Joseph frowned. "But now we'll go slow, to see what is going on."

The jeeps slowed to a crawl before stopping on the top of a ridge so they could see down. The gunfire stopped, but they weren't sure what that meant.

They looked down into the deep canyon and saw ten men in camouflage moving in on three rhinos that were down. These poachers were too far out of range for their rifles. More shots rang out.

One poacher fell. Another fell. Yet a third poacher fell. The rest ran for cover in the nearby trees. A man on horseback seemed to come out of nowhere and gave chase. Black Robin Hood, like most others in the jungle, wore camouflage. He earned his name for his actions, not for the way he dressed.

He disappeared into the forest. The men in the jeeps stayed to watch and listen. For the next half hour, shots continued to ring out. At last, they fell silent.

"You see what I mean about the Black Robin Hood?" Joseph asked with his usual smile. "Shawn in the third jeep is a veterinarian. He has worked on many rhinos, including white rhinos. We will drive down there, see if any of the rhinos are alive and if we can help them."

Joseph led the way in the first jeep. The gunfire had stopped, so they didn't feel any danger, especially since the Wantu were confident that Black Robin Hood had taken care of the poachers. Though the terrain was rough, they tried to get to the rhinos as quickly as possible.

As soon as the jeeps stopped, Shawn jumped out and ran to the rhinos. He took their pulses and felt for injuries. One was dead, but the other two were alive. He put medications in their wounds and bandaged them up. He gave them vaccinations. The two survivors were unconscious, but breathing okay.

Shawn worked his way back to the jeeps. "I've done what I can for now. We don't have the vehicles to move them. All we can do is come back in a day or two and see how they are doing," he reported. "When we come back, if they need it, we can shoot them with anesthesia, then redress their wounds and give them more medicine. For now, we're done."

Joseph looked at Sky. "Shawn does great work. He keeps many of the rhinos and our other special friends alive. He comes out once a month, and when needed. Now, Sky, we turn to you. The other reason I brought you here is because I want you to see a special flower. Here, put this on and let's start walking." Joseph handed Sky a backpack brought especially for him.

"We're going to walk into the jungle just to see a flower?" Sky inquired.

"Not just any flower. It has special qualities. Trust me."

The twenty men hoisted on their packs. They followed a path into the jungle — the same path taken by the poachers, and the one Black Robin Hood used to chase them.

About fifteen minutes in they found a dead poacher. Soon after, two other dead poachers. Before each body was a rope tied between trees used to trip them up. Black Robin Hood had trapped them one by one, caught up to them, and shot them.

They saw the poachers' tracks and the hoofprints from the vigilante's horse, but one hour in, all traces vanished. Not a single track could be found. It was spooky.

They kept walking for another hour. Along the way, colorful birds continued to make noise. All around were the sounds of jungle wildlife.

Joseph stopped and told his men to get the ropes out. Several took out ropes and looped them up a tree to climb.

After the ropes were solid, Joseph, Sky and several of the Wantu climbed about halfway up the tree. Where two branches came together was a small bush with a bright red flower, growing right on the tree. It looked like something from the tulip family.

"Now, isn't that something to see, my friend?" Joseph marveled.

"That is beautiful," Sky agreed.

Joseph plucked it off the branch and handed it to Sky. "Now eat it."

"Eat it?"

"I didn't stutter. *Eat it,*" Joseph repeated.

"Why would I want to eat such a beautiful flower?"

"Because I'm telling you to," Joseph said. "Now eat the damn thing."

Sky could see that Joseph was serious. He bit off a small petal.

"How's it taste?" Joseph asked.

"It's actually got a bit of a sweet taste to it. You mean you haven't tasted it? Do you want a bite?"

Joseph shook his head. He directed that Sky must devour all of it.

"Why on earth?"

"Just eat it. All of it!" he bellowed.

Sky kept chewing away, until within a few minutes the flower was gone.

"Now what?" Sky asked.

"We wait," Joseph responded, "but not here. Let's start getting down."

The group slowly moved down to the ground and started back toward the vehicles.

"I told you that the flower has special powers. It has the power to make people remember whatever they have forgotten," Joseph explained.

Sky laughed.

"You're trying to bring back my memory and that's a great goal, but will it work? How long will it take?" Sky asked, dubious.

"We'll see. Everybody reacts differently."

The walk back to the jeep took two hours, then the drive back to camp. Sky enjoyed the trek because he loved the scenery and sounds of the jungle, so different from anything he had known. Though he didn't have his memory, he did have his mind and his senses.

Back at the Wantu camp the group made a beeline to the community dinner table. The people were dancing; it was a happy time; life was good for all involved.

The day had been a long one, and when Sky at last returned to his rondavel, he hit the sack and slept deeply.

When the sun crept into his room the next morning, he woke to a mind that was bouncing all over. Everything was coming back to him. He looked outside; then he ran to Joseph's home. He found him already waiting.

"It's all coming back to me! My name is Allen Lomayestewa, and I come from the Hopi Nation."

3

Cynthia Baxter

The short blond-haired girl grabbed her dinner from the stove and hastily sat down next to her mom.

"When Dad gets home tonight, you're not gonna fight, are you?"

Susan gave her a half-glare. "I sure hope not, but I can't control that."

"Maybe if you just go along with everything he says, there won't be any problems," said the girl with a flick of her hair.

"Is that what you want?"

"I don't want any of this. But maybe if we just go along, then things will get better."

"Okay, I'll try it, but we'll have to see how it goes."

"Thanks, Mom."

Cynthia's father David strolled in, put his coat on the rack and headed for his chair.

"Get me my beer, wouldya please?" It sounded like an order.

"Sure honey," Susan responded. "How was your day?"

"Just another day at work, you know I don't like to talk about it. Let's talk about anything else."

"Sure honey," she tried again. "What would you like to talk about?"

"I'd *love* to talk about our finances, but since we don't have any, that's probably not a good subject either," he said with a sneer.

The tension was beginning to build. If someone came into their home just now, they might not know what was going on, but they would know that love was not in the air.

"Dad, I got a B on my English composition in school today. I thought that was pretty good," Cynthia said proudly.

"Well, it's good that maybe you'll amount to something more than us," David remarked.

"I think that's great," Susan said quietly.

David picked up the *Arizona Daily Sun,* but winced as he read about the economy.

"I guess I should feel lucky, because there are a lot of people out of work. I work my ass off and can barely keep up. Gas keeps going up. Groceries, up. Everything goes up except my pay, at least not enough to keep up with inflation." He gulped his beer.

Mother and daughter looked at each other without knowing what to say. They wanted to be sympathetic, but knew David would react.

He slapped his hand down hard on the table. "Well, so much for my pep talk."

Cynthia knew it was time to change the conversation. "There's a dance at the high school on Saturday," she began. "Do you think I could go?"

His face softened. "I don't see why not. But who are you gonna go with?"

"Just my regulars, John, Debbie and Natasha," she replied.

"What kind of music will they play?"

"Our normal hip-hop stuff," she answered hopefully.

David made an odd face about the music, but then Susan arrived with plates of food and he was happy for a moment, he could eat and forget his worries.

Settling in to the news and his detective shows, he kept on with his beer, not keeping count and not especially caring.

"Daddy, I love you. I've got to go do my homework," Cynthia told him.

"Okay sweetheart, see you in the morning."

Cynthia disappeared into her bedroom.

"She keeps me going. We've got to do right by my little girl," he stressed.

Susan smiled at him. "That's always my hope." She paused. "I hope she stays on the right path and goes to college," she added, concerned.

David took another swig of beer between reading the paper and watching TV. Susan, for her part, half-watched the show with an eye on her husband to make sure he wouldn't blow up, which could happen at any minute.

Cynthia, meanwhile, did homework for an hour, till she was sure her parents were in bed or sound asleep in the living room with the TV on. She knew they wouldn't check on her. Her father was passed out from the beer, and her mother was dead tired from housework all day and then trying to figure out how to avoid a fight, or a beating.

So, Cynthia did what she did several times a week: went out her window and headed for her friends.

John, Debbie and Natasha were expecting her. The four would meet at either John's or Debbie's two or three times a week. Their parents didn't know and, they thought, probably wouldn't care as long as they felt their kids were safe.

The teenagers would usually drink beer during their gatherings, but nobody would get drunk. They knew they had to go to school the next day and that their only way out of this suffocating environment was good grades, college and finding good jobs.

Sex wasn't any part of their meetings. John was just a friend to all three girls, comfortable hanging out with them and vice versa. All four would have to look elsewhere to meet those needs.

Occasionally they would smoke marijuana to get a few giggles going, to forget for a spell the hard times in their families, but none wanted anything stronger. They would talk about school, the hard subjects, the easy ones, the quirky teachers and all the different students: the nerds, the jocks, the computer geeks, the musicians and the kids who didn't fit in with any of the cliques.

Some of the students stayed in their own cliques, but the four in this group didn't want those limits. They tended to hang with whomever they wanted, at any time.

Cynthia never talked about the violence in her home. She might mention that her parents argued, but she kept mum about her father for two reasons. She didn't want to burden her friends or make them anxious, and she was afraid that they might report the violence. That would certainly cause more problems, and the violence could escalate.

She wanted to finish high school and go off to college to get away from that, to escape. But Cynthia was scared for her mom's safety if she left. She didn't like her options.

Sneaking off didn't impact her grades because she knew that school was her only way out, and she was committed to improving her life.

Cynthia thought about her future and wondered if she would ever marry. She certainly wouldn't tolerate an abuser, but more importantly, she wanted to choose wisely so that she wouldn't end up with one. Did her mom know her dad was an abuser when she married him? Why would she tolerate abuse? When did he cross the line — or was he always like that?

Knowing what she knew about her family, how could she cross over to the other side, the one of peace? How could she make things right in her world; to counteract the ugliness she saw in her dad?

She promised herself not only that would she not hook up with an abuser, but she would commit to being kind and helping others. She would work with the National Honor Society on the food drive for the elderly, and with the local food bank to make sure the poor get fed, and she wanted to work with animals.

On the nights they smoked weed, their custom was to sit in a circle around the table, because they watched *That '70s Show* and thought it would be funny to copy them.

"So, what are you going to major in when you go to college?" John asked Cynthia.

"I'm still considering my options. Maybe I could be a social worker, a fundraiser for nonprofits, or a veterinarian," she said.

"I want to be a nurse," Debbie chimed in. "It's not as much education as a doctor, but you're making good money and helping sick people at the same time."

Natasha said she wanted to be an art teacher. She was good at drawings, paintings and knitting. She sold some, but didn't make much money. She figured if she became an art teacher, that would give her the money to make her own art.

John liked most of his teachers and Natasha's idea of teaching, but he also liked literature and thought about being an English teacher. Northern Arizona University was right in their backyard, but none of these four even considered going there. Each had family issues that motivated them to go elsewhere — maybe not far away; far enough to feel independent, yet close enough to come home if necessary. This was especially true for Cynthia. All believed they wouldn't have much of a future without an education.

The four would share their thoughts, but John was the Firestarter, meaning he would always broach subjects the others would never bring up on their own.

"I'm not usually one to talk politics," John began, "but one of the Navajo students at school was talking to me about the skiing and the wastewater on the San Francisco Peaks. He said it was a sacred place to the Navajo and Hopi, and mainstream society was disrespecting them by using it to make money and for recreation. I never thought about it before, but it seems wrong. Forget about the religious part, because I don't know anything about the Navajo or Hopi religions, but it seems both environmentally and morally wrong that humans of any color would use the mountain this way."

"Wow, that's heavy." Debbie giggled while taking a toke. "I'm going to have to think about that awhile before coming to any decision."

Cynthia looked at John cross-eyed. She didn't know what to think.

Whether in spite of the smoke or because of it, Natasha looked pensive. "It sounds like an interesting topic," she said. "I need to research it. Maybe I can do a paper on it for one of my classes and get extra credit."

"Fair enough," John said.

Debbie and Cynthia agreed they would be open to hearing more.

Now it was getting close to midnight, time to go. They had to be up at seven to get to school by eight, and needed to be alert for their classes.

***

As the students milled around their lockers, John stopped to talk with Zee, the Navajo student who wouldn't stop talking about the issues involved with the San Francisco Peaks. Zee was a nickname, not his real name, because the teens said *zee* when they mean *no*. He was adamant that society should be saying *zee* to the skiing and use of reclaimed water on the peaks.

"Zee, I want to know more about the San Francisco Peaks issue. What do I do?" John asked.

"Here's a copy of the *Navajo-Hopi Observer*. Read about the Peaks. Then google it. There's all kinds of information pro and con about it on the internet. Then there's a meeting this Friday night, so come and check it out."

John was determined to find out if the cause was as righteous as Zee made it sound.

"Those behind the skiing may not be bad people," Zee continued. "They just want to offer some recreation and make some money in the process. But they don't understand Native Americans. They don't respect Native Americans. They also don't respect Mother Earth. They don't see the ills of their ways. They may not be evil. Maybe they're just dumb."

John told Zee he would look into it and get back to him. John knew his friends weren't political, but he also knew they believed in justice, so he wanted to get them involved.

After morning classes, the four friends headed for the cafeteria.

"I need to talk to you guys," John told the girls. "Remember the other night, when I mentioned the San Francisco Peaks? The whole skiing thing, and how they're using reclaimed water — I mean *sewer* water — to make fake snow so people can ski? It's truly gross."

"Oh no, there he goes again!" Natasha giggled.

"Wait a minute. Some issues are worth fighting for," Cynthia said. "We just have to figure out if this is one, we want to put ourselves on the line for."

Debbie repeated she wanted to look into the ski-resort issue before making a decision.

"That's all I'm asking," John said. "This is important. I don't want this to be forgotten. How about tonight we all go together to the library and research it? It would be something different for us to do."

The girls looked at one another.

"I'll bring the weed for the circle later on," he added.

That brought smiles to their faces, and they were in.

"We'll split it up this way," John suggested. "I'll look up all the old articles in the *Daily Sun,* Tasha can look up the *Arizona Republic,* Cynthia can google any information she can find online, and Debbie can look at *Congressional Quarterly,* since it's a federal issue. Let's meet about seven, after we've all had dinner."

The girls nodded and headed off to their afternoon classes, then home for some food and to check in with their parents long enough to let them know they were all right.

Cynthia hoped that her dad wouldn't complicate her evening plans. She walked in the door part scared, part concerned, wondering what would happen.

"Hi Mom!"

"Hi, honey! How was your day?"

"It was good, but we have some homework so we're all meeting at the Flag Library at seven to get caught up," Cynthia said, knowing only some of that was true.

"You sound so responsible as a student!" Susan replied.

David came through the door with his usual dour grimace. Cynthia and Susan looked up at him. He'd already had a drink or two. "Greetings, my happy family. What does a guy have to do to get a beer around here?"

The last thing Susan wanted to do was get him a beer to feed his addiction. What made her even more afraid was *not* getting the beer. That would guarantee a fight. "I'll grab that for you," she said.

Susan wanted to ask him about his day and such, but she knew it would only set him off. "Are there any games on tonight you want to watch?" she asked, apprehensive.

Cynthia watched this quietly. She didn't want to set her father off because she knew her mom would pay the price, but especially not tonight. She needed to get to her meeting. "How's my daddy?" she asked sweetly.

"I'm okay, especially when my angel asks me like that," he responded.

"Daddy, I have some homework to do with my friends at the library tonight. Is that all right?" she wheedled.

Though Susan had already approved it, Cynthia didn't want to spring anything on her dad without his say-so, and Susan intuitively knew why she'd asked. Again, what parents would keep their teenage daughter from going to the library? Yet somehow that wasn't the point.

Susan and David continued to chat, but it was controlled. David was not flying into one of his rages. Cynthia gobbled down dinner, smiled at both parents and went out the door.

The four friends met up at the library, excited to get to learning about the issue and then have their fun in the circle. They sat together at a table and started going through newspapers, journals and web articles.

After an hour, John looked up.

"I've seen enough. The people who are behind the ski lodge want just two things: money, and for visitors to enjoy recreation. You can ask which they want more, but it doesn't matter. Those two things are all that's important. That would be okay if only it didn't degrade the environment and disrespect many Native people who consider the mountain sacred."

"When was the last time you were up on the mountain?" Natasha asked.

"Huh." He thought about it. "It's been years."

"How can you expect to be taken seriously if you haven't been on the mountain in years, or even visited the ski resort?" Natasha wanted to know.

"You make a good point," John said, a bit dejectedly. "Okay, we need to go. How about tomorrow after school?"

The girls looked to one another, knowing a decision had to be made. If nothing else it meant they would go somewhere they hadn't been for a while, maybe even find an adventure or two. "We're in," they said at once.

The foursome stood up. "I always make good on my promises," John said.

Soon they were puffing and giggling in the circle.

***

"Maybe we should monkey-wrench it." Debbie laughed.

"What's that?" Natasha asked.

"There's this author Edward Abbey, and when his characters didn't like something, a company was doing because it hurt the environment, they would *monkey-wrench* it, meaning they would vandalize the vehicles doing the work," Debbie explained.

Natasha shook her head. "I'm not ready for that. I could go to jail for that and it could mess up my future."

John agreed that monkey-wrenching was not the way they wanted to go. "You don't have to vandalize a place to oppose it. That might not do any good anyway, because people look down on it." He elaborated, "There's a process. You take your issue to the public. You take your issue to the City Council, the state legislature and Congress. There's a lot of ways to fight something."

"How do you know it'll work?" Natasha asked.

"You have to have faith," he replied. "But it doesn't happen overnight; no big issue is won or lost that way. It will take years, maybe decades. It's a matter of perseverance."

"Well, aren't *you* the politician!" Debbie remarked.

"The Peaks issue is new to me, but I've been studying politics for years and learning how to attack issues that people care about," John responded.

Debbie put the conversation back on track. "Okay, okay, we get it," she said. "I'm ready to go home, but let's go up to the peaks tomorrow."

All agreed, and the four headed to their respective homes. Cynthia was excited about the prospect of seeing the Peaks, of getting more involved and backing an important environmental issue. Her first concern, though, was what she would find when she got home.

If everybody was asleep, she could sleep through another night without fear. She knew all too well there were other possibilities.

Sure enough, when she entered the house, she could hear fighting in the kitchen — or rather, a habitual abuser taking shots at his beaten-down wife.

"Dirty fat whore! You are *so stupid*. I don't know why I even have to look at you …," he continued to berate her.

Cynthia hated her father for this. She wished her mom would call the police or leave, to get away from him. Of course, if her parents split, she would stick with Susan even if that meant living on the streets.

She knew well, though, that her mom couldn't just leave, no matter how much she wanted to, as a matter of her own and her daughter's safety. David controlled her and kept her from working — for so long, she would have a hard time getting a job.

Cynthia wanted to call the police. *Better not.* She didn't know how David might respond. Anything could happen.

"You better do what I tell you to, bitch, or you'll regret it. You know what I'll do," she heard him threaten.

Neither parent knew that she was home. David was too busy yelling, and Susan was too busy being terrorized. Though the abuse had gone on for years, Cynthia herself was spared the same ill treatment, which confused her. Why the difference? Why not her as well?

Too many nights, feeling powerless, Cynthia would just put her head in her pillow and cry — but not this time. Tonight, she would take action. She knew that her mere presence might alter his behavior — so why not change the channel? With that in mind, she strode into the kitchen and blurted out, "I want a baloney sandwich."

"Ah, my little angel," David responded, right on cue.

"Yes Daddy. How is your night?" she asked, feigning innocence.

"Better now that you're here," he said sweetly.

"Would you come talk to me, Daddy?" she began.

"Of course! What would you like to talk about?"

"Come to my room and I'll tell you."

"Okay."

Susan took her cue as well. "I'm going to bed," she announced with a smile as David followed Cynthia to her room.

"Daddy, what do you think of the fake snow on the San Francisco Peaks?" she started.

"It's a crime, a damn crime. But it's business, and that's hard to stop."

"I feel the same way, but I want to do what I can to stop it. My friends and I have been talking about it," she continued.

"That's good! I didn't say it *couldn't* be done. I'm not telling you to give up. Just letting you know you have a long road to go."

"Thanks for the pep talk!"

"Now, you get a good night's sleep so you can approach this with a clear head tomorrow," he said. "My angel." He kissed her on the forehead and headed off to bed.

She let out a sigh of relief. David would go to sleep without bothering Susan. And her mom, she knew, would have a chance at sleep if she didn't have to worry about him tomorrow. She'd defused the bomb.

Cynthia felt alone in the world. Not that she was lacking in either friends or a future, but rather in the stubborn feeling that of all of the families, hers was the worst. She didn't know of anyone else her age who had to worry whether Dad was about to beat up Mom. It could happen anytime, in any moment.

She promised herself over and over not to ever let that happen to her. If and when she met a boy she liked, she would certainly take her time to get to know him. No rushed engagement or pressure to marry. She had to be *sure* he wasn't an abuser.

She dreamed of someone who would be gentle, considerate and kind, someone with whom she could feel safe sleeping at night. She was exhausted by thoughts about the Peaks and her father. Now she could drift off to sleep in hopes that tomorrow she might find at least some peace and adventure on the road trip to Snowbowl.

***

That day, though excited about their trip, the four remained focused on their classes. Keeping their grades up was important. If they became involved in the Snowbowl issue, they didn't want anything on their record for critics to use against them.

As soon as school ended, the friends met up in the school parking lot at John's Chevy Cobalt. They piled in all smiles, glad to be going someplace they hadn't been in a while.

They took Route 160 to Snowbowl Road, which goes up the mountain. The resort is surrounded by the Coconino National Forest, one of the largest pine forests in the world. They were awed by the greenery.

They noticed two things on their way up the mountain: ugly black pipes that carried reclaimed water for the snow machines, and signs posted on some of the trees about a protest taking place on Saturday against the use of the reclaimed water. As they pulled in to park, they could see a Snowbowl worker removing the signs.

A parking lot below was for hiking trails. To the right, hikers would find the Kachina Trail, and to the left, the Agassiz Trail, which leads to the top of the peaks — the highest point in Arizona, at more than 12,000 feet. They decided to park by the Agassiz Trail and walk a few minutes across the meadow, where they were stunned by the panorama: a dozen different types of flowers and Arizona scenery that boggled the mind.

"This is beautiful! How can anyone desecrate this place in any way?" Cynthia wondered out loud.

"It does look like a place worth fighting for. I can see why Native people, or anyone, would find this place sacred," John agreed.

The four sat mesmerized by the beauty.

"Wow, this is something. I don't know how I could possibly describe this to my relatives who haven't been here," Debbie said.

John responded that they could talk to Zee and others already involved in trying to save the Peaks, but it was clear that they should attend Saturday's protest.

They sat for a long time. Sometimes they would talk softly or giggle, but mostly they wanted to soak it all in.

"We have to do this more often," Cynthia said.

"We'll do the protest, and probably be up here a lot more just dealing with the issue, but Cynthia is right. This place is wonderful and coming up here will help us forget about those parts of life we want to escape."

They were up about 9,000 feet, so the September air kept them cool, but it wasn't cold yet. They felt just right, and that their decision to join the battle to protect the Peaks was righteous. Each was excited to have an issue to work on that would make them proud, and to have found another place to come for their sanctuary.

Hours passed. The sun was starting down. The cool air was turning colder, but didn't dim the wondrous beauty. Having made the most of this day, they headed home, knowing Saturday would come quickly.

***

The next day they made a point of meeting with Zee at school. He was all smiles as they told him all about their trip.

"Yeah, the Peaks is a magical place, but it's also a sacred place to the Navajo, Hopi and other tribes," Zee told them. "So, you're coming to the protest on Saturday?"

"Now we wouldn't miss it for the world!" John replied.

School that Friday went by quickly. They went to their classes and did their work quietly, saving their energy for the following day. Friday night was typically reserved for their get-together, but this night was different. No one wanted to miss the protest. Each headed home and made sure to turn in early.

The protest was scheduled for 10am. They met up at John's at 8:15, went downtown for coffee, then headed for Snowbowl.

On arrival, they could already see the media trucks. Two of the network TV stations from Phoenix were there to cover the event, along with NAZ-TV from Northern Arizona University. Flagstaff's *Arizona Daily Sun* reporter was also making her way toward the crowd. Aware that Zee was one of the leaders, most of the media rushed to interview him.

"It's a travesty what they've done up here, and they need to be stopped," he told them.

In the background, protesters chanted, "Hey hey, ho ho, Snow-bowl has got to go!"

Snowbowl workers watched from the deck of the restaurant, with law enforcement that included city, county and state police fully visible.

Snowbowl too had its own security guards, who monitored the protesters and took notes and photos. The protesters would smile for the cameras, regardless of who was taking their picture. They weren't hiding. They were proud they were there to make their presence and feelings known.

A Snowbowl representative was there as well, to inform the media that he respected the religious beliefs of others, but that the Snowbowl people had their rights too, to build their business and bring recreation to make people happy. He added that the environmental concerns were bogus, that the US Forest Service had done several studies and the impact to the environment was rated as negligible.

The foursome joined in marching and chanting. They were glad the media people weren't talking to them, because they were new to the issue. They felt strongly about their stance, but uncertain they could articulate their views in a way that would sound rational to listeners.

The protesters were careful not to bring booze or drugs, or do anything out of line. They knew the public was watching and that if they broke the law, their messaging would be compromised. Acting within the bounds of the law clearly doesn't guarantee acceptance, but it meant they had a better chance of getting people to listen.

The media took turns interviewing leaders and other protesters at random. They interviewed Snowbowl employees and customers as well. Law enforcement stood eagle-eyed to maintain security and ensure no laws were broken.

After a couple hours, the protesters felt they made their point and that their work was done for the day.

John went up to Zee. "I feel like I had fun today, but I also felt that I was doing something righteous — something I could feel good about, although I'm not sure it's gonna do any good."

Zee responded that John was right, that they were taking the right action regardless of the outcome. "We're doing the right thing, but I don't know what the courts will decide. Court decisions seem arbitrary — they depend on who the judge is, on who appointed them. They call it justice, but the system seems like it's always rigged."

John nodded. The four headed for the car. All were smiling because they felt they did something good and that they were among friends.

"Well, we should have the circle this afternoon to talk about this," Natasha said.

Cynthia giggled. "Not gonna argue with that!"

Debbie offered that they could go to her house since her parents were out shopping.

Half an hour later they were lighting up in their circle.

"Those cops made me feel creepy. The way they were staring at us made me feel icky," said Natasha.

"Maybe, Tasha, but they didn't harass anybody. They didn't say anything bad about our cause. We couldn't really tell whether they were for us or against us," John said.

Cynthia nodded. "They're not our problem. Our problem is the people at Snowbowl who want to make money and all the skiers who couldn't care less about other people or the environment as long as they have their fun."

Debbie admitted she was too busy looking at all the cute boys to pay attention to what the cops were doing. John rolled his eyes.

The foursome went on chatting about high school, politics, sports and music, the girls sometimes drifting into talk about clothes and makeup, which left John feeling a little weird about being the only boy present.

At around 4:30 Cynthia said she had to be getting back. She wanted to be home in time for the five-o'clock news to see how it covered the protest.

David was in his chair as usual, reading the newspaper with the TV on. Susan was in the kitchen cooking dinner.

"There she is! How'd the protest go?" he asked.

"Well, Daddy, we got our message out, I just don't know who's listening or whether anyone plans to do anything about it."

"I know how you feel. We go through life believing in justice and fairness, but sometimes it doesn't work out that way, and we just have to be prepared for it," he said.

Cynthia asked him to flip to the news, and he did, not just to make his daughter happy. He also wanted to see if the cameras caught her at the protest.

The lead story was about an NFL player who'd punched out his girlfriend. The piece segued into a broader segment on domestic violence.

"One in four women in America suffers from domestic violence. One in 13 Arizona women is murdered. For help, the National Domestic Violence Hotline is 928-799-7233, and the Arizona Domestic Violence Hotline is 800-782-6400 ...."

At that David was unusually quiet. Cynthia saw at once that she was far from alone on this issue, yet the report didn't make her feel any better.

The counselor on camera spoke about how domestic violence impacts both rich and poor, and that it doesn't discriminate on the basis of race: that when it comes to domestic violence, all are equally susceptible.

Cynthia debated whether she should call the hotline, but she was scared not only for her mother and herself, but for her dad as well. She had seen too many news reports about wives and children being killed — and then the men killing themselves — when their families contacted law enforcement.

She didn't think David would do that, but then again, she never imagined him capable of abusing her mom as he had in recent years.

David got up to go to the bathroom, muttering something about law enforcement minding its own business when it comes to family matters. Cynthia breathed a sigh. She didn't know if the news would cause him to erupt; anything could touch him off, especially a subject as touchy as this.

The newscaster announced the Snowbowl protest next, after the break. A clip of the protesters in front of the Snowbowl building appeared briefly before they cut to the commercial. Cynthia called her dad to tell him the segment would be on any minute.

Both were eager to watch it. Cynthia hugged her pillow while David laid back in his recliner. The newscaster gave a balanced report, beginning with the protesters and following up with the Snowbowl supporters, each with equal time to express their views.

"There you are!" David shouted, pointing to his daughter in the background, holding a sign. He seemed proud of his young righteous rebel.

"Come in, Mom! You gotta see this!" Cynthia yelled.

Susan came running, excited to see her daughter on TV. Cynthia had thought twice about calling her in — she didn't want to put her in the same room as Dad, afraid her mother might set him off.

"Look at you!" Susan beamed. "We have a movie star in the family. I'm glad you're standing up for what you believe in."

"That's my angel," David chimed in.

The evening ended peacefully with David acting calmly and not throwing any tantrums.

Cynthia enjoyed the calm that night, rare enough in this household. She went to sleep feeling righteous about her cause, happy and grateful for her parents' support and supremely relieved that they didn't fight. She hoped that tomorrow would bring more of the same, but a small voice inside said, *don't count on it*.

***

On Monday morning, the four friends met in the school cafeteria to munch out, discuss the protest and talk about what's next.

Zee came running over.

"Did you see the news?" He saw the blank looks on their faces. "The Supreme Court ruled against the Native Americans again! It's like the religion of the Native Americans doesn't count when it goes up against American recreation and business. Money talks!"

"So, do we just give up?" Cynthia asked.

"No way," Zee responded. "Our supporters will back politicians who'll stand up for us. Then the lawyers will see if they can find a way to take it back to the courts. It can take years, but there's always a way."

"Sounds like a frustrating process for those who believe in the cause," Cynthia said.

"Sure, but fighting for the good guys often takes time. Look how long it took to free the slaves, for women to get the vote, for the Jews to overcome the Holocaust. Like they say, freedom isn't necessarily free." Zee continued. "The Peaks are just one of many issues worth fighting for, and sometimes we win. Take the proposal to mine uranium in the Grand Canyon: that's been a battle for years. You'd think that no one would want to violate the Grand Canyon like that — one of the Seven Wonders of the World. But for some, the money and jobs mean more than respecting the environment. The Court, though, has continually ruled in our favor, against allowing the mining of uranium there."

"I never thought of it in those terms." Cynthia paused. "You think about a lot of issues, don't you?"

"Speaking of issues, Andrew Walden is giving a talk at Northern Arizona this weekend. This guy has traveled all over Africa. He's taken some beautiful photos of the scenery and wildlife, but he also speaks out about poaching because there's a lot of poachers in Africa who sell the skins and horns for food or for use in their ceremonies," Zee told them.

Cynthia thought the photos sounded nice, but that the issues were heavy. "Still, we need to check it out," she said.

The four agreed they would go to the Africa presentation, but they also needed to stay focused on school. College loomed.

"I want to go to Walnut Canyon today after school," Cynthia said. "We haven't been there for a while, and I want to get back there before it gets too cold."

***

On the way to Walnut Canyon and its hiking trails, Cynthia thought about the contrast between rich and poor. On the drive they would pass by the country club and its subdivision. Only wealthy people lived here, while a ten-minute drive away in Mobile Haven it was poor folks. Yet, regardless of income, if you had a car or could hitchhike, you could find your way to Walnut Canyon and lose yourself in nature.

They rarely took the main entrance. Instead, they would get on the Fisher Point Hiking Trail and find a back way into the canyon. That way they could avoid the crowds and paying the fee.

They appreciated the ancient cliff dwellings for which the canyon is so well known, but even more, here the four could find quiet. Here was a place away from the crowd, beautiful in its own special way.

The cold hadn't yet set in for the winter, and many of the trees still had their leaves. The friends loved going up and down the steep trails. They enjoyed the sandstone and limestone.

Indian paintbrush, columbine and daisies were just some of the flowers that would tantalize them. Those times when they would see deer or wild turkey were special, along with sightings of favorite birds and their calls, especially the blue jays.

Once at the canyon, they used their smartphones to google Dr. Andrew Walden. At first, they couldn't believe how beautiful his photos were of the African jungle, the astonishing animals and multicolored birds of that faraway place.

Then the photographs turned ugly. Walden posted pictures of what the big game looked like after they'd been savaged by poachers.

"It's eye-opening." Cynthia gasped. "Look at the beauty of these pictures," she pointed, "and the ugliness of those. I can't believe this came from the same person, in the same place!"

John looked at her, pensive. "You're right," he said. "It just shows there is good and bad in this world. You have to enjoy the good and do what you can to fight the bad."

It was getting dark. They wanted to stay forever but knew that the cold air was coming. They didn't want to get back their families, but homework was their only way out, so they had to stay focused.

***

Saturday arrived, and with-it Walden's Africa presentation. The place was packed with NAU students who were there for the environment, tribal cultures or both.

He didn't disappoint. Walden spent the first hour going through PowerPoint slides and talking about the beauty of the African landscape, the wild animals and the tribal people. Then, in the second hour, he switched abruptly to the shocking photos of big wild animals that had been poached.

The usually loud students went quiet, except for some who reacted with noisy whispers of *That's gross!* Others turned away, unable to bear to watch the bloody slideshow.

"I show you this not to gross you out or get you upset, though it *is* upsetting," Walden explained. "I show you this as a call to action. This place is thousands of miles away from you. I realize that most of you can't just jump on a flight to Africa. But you can join this battle." He continued. "You can help fund our battle against the poachers. You can write your representatives and senators to tell them to take action against the poachers through diplomacy. So, I ask you to join us!"

The crowd applauded.

Following the brief meet-and-greet with Walden and the other environmentalists in the crowd, the foursome started toward the exit and the car.

"I'd love to go to Africa and see all those cool big animals," Natasha said. "But I don't know if I could deal with the heartbreak of looking at the ones that get killed."

"Oh, come on, put on your big-girl pants, Tasha!" Debbie said. "How is the world ever going to solve any problems if everybody is too afraid to deal with the issues that have to be dealt with?"

"I like what you're saying, but we have so many problems here in Flagstaff, in Arizona and the rest of America. We don't have to go to another country to solve problems," John said. "Let's look at this situation practically. First, we'd have to get passports to go to another country. Then we'd have to raise thousands of dollars for each of us who's going. If we're going to raise money, why don't we raise money here for the local food bank, the Sierra Club or any of the issues here where we live?"

Cynthia rolled her eyes. "If I have a passion and it's in another country, another continent, you're going to tell me I still have to stay here to deal with the issues here? That's crap! I should be able to follow my dreams wherever they take me."

They could see that the evening was a little much for them to take in. They each had some thinking to do.

"Speaking of our dreams. Isn't this our night to smoke up?" Cynthia asked.

The four broke out in big smiles and headed for the car.

During the circle they avoided any further talk about going to Africa. Instead, they went back to dishing about students and teachers at their high school, the better to lighten the mood.

When Cynthia got home, she could hear her parents arguing in the kitchen. That wasn't unusual, but this sounded different. More serious.

"You little slut *whore*, you can't do anything right, you dumb *stupid* ass!" David was yelling.

Susan was crying. It was more a private sobbing, of someone completely alone and afraid for her health and safety. Cynthia knew at once that anything her mother might say could set him off and end up that much worse for her — a worse beating, more physical pain and abuse.

Tonight felt as though some threshold had been crossed. Susan sat slumped, and apart from her sobbing, she remained deathly quiet.

Cynthia was scared. What should she do? Just avoid the situation? If she took that strategy and her mom was seriously hurt, she would never forgive herself; but if she intervened in some way that her dad didn't like, things could get so much worse.

Cynthia waltzed into the kitchen as though nothing was going on.

"Hi Mom and Dad, I'm home! I'm hungry. I think I'll make myself some dinner," she tried.

"Not now, angel." David told her. "We're having an adult discussion and we need to finish it. You go to your room now and when we're done, I'll let you know so you can get that dinner,"

Cynthia just barely glanced at her mom. She didn't want to give him any idea that she knew what was going on. The glimpse of Susan showed swollen eyes. *Is that from crying — or did he hit her?*

"Okay, Daddy," she said.

Cynthia left the kitchen, but as soon as the door closed, she put her ear up against it. She heard a smack. The sobbing became louder.

"All I do is work and work! All you do is stay home, watch your stupid soap operas and lounge around like this is a damn country club," he raged.

Cynthia cracked the kitchen door just enough to see inside. David raised his arm and struck Susan backhand with all his might. He was much taller and stronger, and she went flying: her face hit the sink full of pots and pans, cutting her face. He also wore a big ring that cut her face as well.

That was all Cynthia could take. Beside herself with fear and worry, she dashed up to her bedroom and immediately dialed 911. Then she eyed the window.

"There's a fight going on at 910 Green Planet Road!" she told the emergency operator and hung up. Then she turned her phone off so the police couldn't call her back.

***

Cynthia sat and waited, staring into the dark, afraid. What would happen to her parents? Would her dad go to jail and come back even worse? Would they haul Susan off as well, since police often don't know which one to believe? Will they take her to a safe house, or the hospital? *Will the police come for me, and make me go to a foster home?*

Cynthia started to cry. The fear was becoming too much — but then she knew she had to pull herself together, for the sake of her mom. Before she could think much more, she heard the police arrive. From her bedroom window, she saw them get out of their vehicles and enter the house. She was afraid that David would start fighting with them. Grabbing a blanket off the bed, she wrapped herself up in it, too fearful to go downstairs. She would listen. Listen and wait. She couldn't hear what they were saying, but she did hear some clattering. She looked out the window again: an ambulance had pulled up, amid a sea of flashing red and blue lights.

Soon, the EMTs had Susan on a gurney and were placing her into the back of the ambulance. As soon as it drove off, the police emerged from the house with David in cuffs. It was over, at least for tonight.

They were gone. Cynthia grabbed the house keys, locked up and headed straight for Debbie's. She would need a ride to the hospital, to check on her mom.

4

PoRue Kazzie

PoRue Kazzie looked up, bewildered. "I don't understand. The elders tell us to respect Mother Earth, yet we look around the villages and all we see is trash. There is illegal dumping that nobody does anything about. There are household goods that people just toss out their door or window. How can this be?"

Her mother Sacheen looked outside as though she wanted to avoid the question. It was starting to rain, with thunder and lightning. Rain is important to Hopis because the more it rains, the better the crops. This storm, though, brought strong wind, which meant that people's trash and outside debris would blow from house to house, yard to yard. It wouldn't be a pretty sight in the morning.

"I'm going to see if I can get a group of kids together from school to do a village cleanup," PoRue said.

"See, you *can* do something about the situation," Sacheen encouraged her.

"But it can't be just us kids. We need to get adults involved. How can we get the principal involved when he's not even from here? How do we get adults involved when they have their own issues to deal with?" PoRue asked.

Sacheen looked at her daughter with pride. She knew PoRue was trying to do something for her community, her people and Mother Earth.

"I don't have all the answers," she said. "But you can't get ahead of yourself by trying to do too much at one time. I'm not saying *don't* do it; you *should* do it. But I'm saying that you have to take one step at a time. You can't do it alone. Get the help of your friends at school, but you have to talk to village leaders and maybe the Tribal Council too."

PoRue asked why they always have to have the permission of the adults. "Why don't we just clean it up ourselves?"

"That's one way to respond," Sacheen answered, in a tone neither supportive nor opposed.

PoRue took a tangent: "I wonder what role the drinking plays in the trash?"

"Huh?"

"When people drink, they don't clean up after each other. They don't seem to care about whether they're littering. They don't seem to care much about anything. All they care about is getting a buzz." PoRue frowned. "They're certainly not going to clean up litter — theirs or anyone else's — while they're getting drunk."

Sacheen could feel her daughter's frustration. She was proud she raised a daughter who was concerned not only about Mother Earth but also about her people and doing the right thing, about having a moral compass.

PoRue said that she cared about other environmental issues, too. That protecting the San Francisco Peaks, for example, should be a priority. That nuclear power plants should be protested. "Yet how can I make those statements to non-Hopis when we aren't showing that we respect our own land?"

Sacheen called that a great question, but again emphasized that she shouldn't get ahead of herself, to take one step at a time and approach the problem with respect for her elders.

PoRue was on a mission, however, that included more than one concern. While the environment was important, social justice mattered, too. She was concerned about how non-Indians had a habit of saying 'redskins.' She was concerned about poverty, how some people could possess so much while so many others struggle to pay their rent, get proper medical care or eat healthy.

"Mom, another thing that bothers me is the car accidents," PoRue continued. "They are the number-one killer on the reservation and border towns. Sure, I know we worry about contaminated water and long-term effects of exposure in the uranium mines, but what about now? What do we do to stop the car accidents — and about the alcohol and drugs that fuel them?"

She could see PoRue was serious. "Why don't you use your photo talents?"

"What? How do you mean?" PoRue asked.

"Well, you're always talking about how much you love photography and you're always taking all these photos. Why don't you put it to some practical use?"

"Oh, I get it! I can take photos of car accidents *and* I can take photos of things that impact the environment. Hmm … this could cost money. How would I pay for gas to go places, and the printing of the photos and use of computers?"

"I'm not sure, dear. About the car accidents, maybe the newspapers or insurance companies would be interested. And about the environmental photos, maybe the government or magazines? Remember, where there's a will, there's a way."

PoRue's friends appreciated her passion about the environment, but their concerns were elsewhere. Kristal Lomayaoma was keen on special education. Millicent Rushoff's focus was on social justice.

Straight-A student Kristal never looked down on those who weren't great with their schoolwork. She had a big heart for students with disabilities, too. She would go with them to Special Olympics and other events for support and encouragement. Though she didn't have relatives with disabilities, she was drawn to those who needed help.

Millie had a different personality. Her emphasis was not so much on getting good grades as on social justice. She didn't like it when she saw on the news that someone was mistreated because they were different. She would stand up for anyone who was a target of abuse, especially when the cause was a difference in skin color, religion or gender. She believed that people should be treated kindly, period.

Millie wanted to localize those feelings too, meaning that if anything was wrong at her school or in her community — a student bullying another student, a principal mistreating a teacher or a teacher mistreating a student — she had to speak out. This meant frequent trips to the principal's office, where she would clue him in on what she considered injustices.

On one level, Principal Glenn Johnson appreciated Millie, but he would typically roll his eyes when he saw her coming, because he knew it meant more work. Her appearance in his office had become part of his day.

Kristal loved the special-education kids. One thing she liked best about them is that they were easier to make smile. Any little compliment or bit of fun would bring them out, and they would shine. They had the ability to be kind to others and to appreciate any kindness sent their way.

Yet she also knew that their disabilities could frustrate them when they found they were unable to reach certain goals. That's why Kristal loved Special Olympics. It gave these students the pleasure of competing and showed how much they could accomplish.

***

The three girls were friends. They even had a breakfast club at school. Each day, before class, they would meet in the math teacher's room.

Mr. Bender, the teacher, would leave them to themselves while he went about his business. (It wasn't really breakfast either, although the girls would sometimes bring burritos from home or buy them from kids who were selling them in the hallways, even though it was against school rules.)

After they exchanged morning greetings, PoRue began.

"Have you heard the Facebook drama with all the pregnancy stories?"

Kristal and Millie exchanged looks.

"Of course," Kristal responded. "Kirsta said Missy was pregnant. Missy said Charlene is pregnant. Charlene said Ryan has VD. Usually, the girls spreading the rumors are the ones who are actually pregnant."

Millie said she was glad that none of *them* was pregnant, and grateful that they as a group would never stoop to spreading rumors about other girls, even those they didn't get along with. Most of the dirt involved high-school girls fighting over boys — but not all of it.

Some of the trash talk being digitally shared typically involved competitions, like who would get the votes to serve as captain of the cheerleaders or president of the National Honor Society.

Inevitably such battles would devolve into shaming on social media — slut-shaming the girls accused of sleeping around or stealing a boyfriend, fat-shaming those who don't have the right figure, gay-shaming others for their orientation, special-education–shaming anyone classified as a remedial student. The list seemed endless. The capacity of teenagers to make up stories and spread them if someone made them mad had no bounds.

PoRue shook her head.

"It's not right that kids make stuff up. It's just mean, and somebody has to stop it," she declared.

Certain students, though, would get their revenge one way or another. If not on social media, sometimes it would come at school and cause a fight.

"Did you hear what Kaine did?" Millie began.

Her friends shook their heads.

"You know how Kaine always says that he doesn't get mad, he gets even?" she continued.

They looked at her, intrigued.

"Well, you know how that older guy Bert was bullying him?"

They nodded.

"Well, Kaine hacked into some shady guy's account, and then put fifty thousand dollars of it into Bert's bank account. He left tracks, not to himself, of course. Bert didn't have a clue. Two men showed up at Bert's house after dark and beat him, almost killed him. Then they made him pay them back or they really truly would have killed him."

Kristal and PoRue looked on in shock, not knowing what to do or say.

***

The trio had a fourth sometimes friend, Mikele Yazzie, who wore a cowboy hat much larger than his head.

Mikele was a true cowboy in the sense that he loved horses and knew how to talk to them. The girls weren't necessarily into cowboys or rodeos, but he seemed to have a gentle spirit that intrigued them. He also had a sarcastic sense of humor that they loved.

One time Mikele took them to his parents' ranch on the outskirts of Flagstaff. The horses would run right up to him — not unusual for anyone who feeds them, but this was different. The horses would snuggle up to his jacket. Mikele would put his face right up against the horses' faces. The horses then would put their nostrils up to his and breathe into them. He would do the same into theirs. It was some kind of funky man-horse bonding.

The girls would exchange looks. They didn't think it was creepy, it was just different from anything they'd ever seen.

"That's unique," PoRue said with a strange expression.

Mikele never tried to hit on any of the three. He liked the friendship and didn't want to do anything that might jeopardize it. He liked the way everything was just fine.

One other thing they shared was their love for the environment and animals.

Mikele heard about horses running wild in Cave Creek. Those untamed creatures had been living on that land for hundreds of years. It was public land, and the Forest Service considered the horses a nuisance. They wanted to round them up and send them off to slaughter.

Mikele found this objectionable.

"Something has to be done," he told the girls. "We can't let these horses be slaughtered."

They joined a group that protested getting rid of the horses. They wrote letters to the newspapers, to the Forest Service and their congressmen. They raised a ruckus, and eventually the Forest Service threw up its hands in frustration and tabled the matter indefinitely. It showed that sometimes activism works.

Mikele was persuasive through the girls' letter-writing campaign, and they were impressed how he was able to have an impact on the issue.

PoRue became the group's social director, organizer and environmental leader. Social in the sense that she was always coming up with things for them to do, whether that involved going to a school dance, a basketball game, a movie or a political or environmental speech, 'organizer' in the sense that everything always had to be clean and tidy. If papers were scattered around, she would put them in files so that anyone could find them at a moment's notice. She would also have the group attend meetings about the ski resort, global warming and protecting the area's water.

***

PoRue found out about Prescott College teacher Andrew Walden speaking at NAU and giving a slideshow about Africa and its wildlife. Her interest in photography put this high on her list to attend and drag her friends along.

"This is something we can really enjoy," she urged. "It's not as serious as someone desecrating a sacred mountain or ruining the air or water. We can just have fun and enjoy the beauty!"

Kristal shrugged.

"I'm not sure how exciting that sounds, but anything to get me out of the house. Hopefully we can go somewhere well to eat, before or after."

"Count me in," Millie said, happy to have another night out with her friends.

"I'll leave that to you girls," Mikele said. "I have to check on my horses Saturday morning."

***

The girls had trouble getting there on time. As much as they wanted to see the African safari presentation, they were running late.

The room could fit about 200 people, and it was packed, not just with environmentalists, but all sorts of others too.

The lights dimmed, and without any introduction, Professor Walden started the slideshow. It began with the moon over African waters, with African music playing and dancers in the foreground. This went on for about fifteen minutes.

Touched and drawn in by the landscape, the audience soon learned about many African cultures. They learned as well about lions, elephants and rhinos, and their importance to the ecosystem of Africa. With much oohing and aahing among the cheerful, happy audience.

Then came one quick slide that read *"Warning: this is about poaching, and it is brutal to watch."* Guns cracked, saws buzzed, shouting carried on, and then the bloodbath: gruesome photos of animals torn to shreds, cut up, mutilated, skinned and left to die. The crowd went silent. The three girls, on the verge of tears, looked sadly at one another.

Walden stopped the slideshow. He talked to the audience about how rhino horns and animal parts were sold on the black market for huge profits. This gave poor Africans an incentive to put their lives on the line and risk poaching, just to earn a living.

"What can be done?" Walden asked the audience. He told them how several African tribes hired rangers to fight off the poachers. While successful to some degree, their success had been spotty; some countries fight off poachers better than others. Rangers have been killed. Poaching slowed, but it didn't stop.

"This is a war we *can* win," he said. "But it will take a lot of work."

He went on to say he understood that most would not be able to go to Africa, yet there was still plenty they could do. He outlined ways in which they could help, such as donating money or writing government officials to do what they could about the dire situations.

He led photo safaris to Congo, he explained, where they could learn more, but the cost was about $10,000 per person for a two- to three-week tour. During these safaris they would meet with African leaders and rangers, as well as local people who would tell them how they could get involved in the fight.

The three girls shared a look that said they wanted to join the cause — but where to start?

Walden took questions from the audience, then told them that refreshments were available in the back of the room, where he would be happy to chat with anyone who wanted to learn more. PoRue, Kristal and Millie approached.

"We want to go to Africa with you," PoRue blurted out, not quite realizing what she'd said.

Kristal and Millie looked more than a little astonished that if PoRue was ready, she hadn't even said a word — and now, here they were, standing before this man Walden. What in the world could be next?

5

Kyle Tsinnie

For Kyle Tsinnie, age nineteen, high-school graduation was a turning point. A bit more than a year before, his whole world changed due to COVID.

This young man from Tuba City was unique in one respect: he was the only Navajo who was serious about breaking into the world of auto racing.

The coronavirus outbreak impacted him more than most because the Navajo Nation was one of America's hottest spots. He was fortunate in that no one in his family had the virus, yet here, among the Navajos, he knew many who did — some of whom died.

Kyle had started racing cars at age sixteen. Following the outbreak, the racing world changed. He saw races canceled, or those with only a limited audience and some with no audience at all. The window was fast closing on his future, or so it seemed. He was glad, then, to see Phoenix Raceway return to full capacity, though that too changed due to the new safety protocols.

These changes coincided with nationwide protests against police brutality and racism. This affected Kyle's world, too. The lone Black driver on the racing circuit, for example, found slurs spray-painted on his car in the park's garage. His racing colleagues marched in support, a show of kinship and solidarity for their fellow driver.

A nearby synagogue was vandalized that same night. That the two incidents were connected remained unclear; without evidence, a guess could be made either way, but the timing raised suspicions that were hard to quell.

While Black Lives Matter and synagogue protesters did show up at some of the races, slowing traffic in places, the protests were peaceful and didn't garner much media attention.

It concerned him, though, that if he became a successful driver, he'd have to worry about how people would respond to a Navajo's success.

This gave Kyle pause for thought about what's important in life. Family had to come first. His parents and, maybe even more importantly, his grandparents and other elders spoke often about the importance of family.

After family, racing was second. After that, everything came in a distant third. Education for him was a case in point: it was important in that the elders encouraged him to go to college, get an education and come back to help their people, but his dream of racing trumped all that.

Unlike most boys his age, for Kyle, girlfriends were not important. Most of his high-school buddies had girlfriends, but he felt they were nothing but distraction.

Drugs and alcohol were distractions too, common in his community and among some of his friends. When offered, Kyle's response would be to count him out. "When you're racing a car at more than two hundred miles per hour," he'd tell them, "a mistake can be deadly." He was focused on racing. It was his love, his obsession.

He was a food and exercise guru. Driving at high speed takes arm and leg strength, as well as good reflexes. For energy he needed protein, and he supplemented a healthy diet with a range of fruits and vegetables. Not much fry bread here.

Exercise meant running, a long-observed tradition among the Navajo. It meant working the legs on a bicycle as well, and working the arms on machines. Kyle's goals and workout regimen were well known in various communities. Many of the younger kids looked up to him, and the schools called him in to speak sometimes.

While friendly with everybody in Tuba City, Kyle wasn't especially close with anyone his own age there. He sorted his classmates into three categories: jocks, nerds and druggies, and he didn't feel he fit in with any of them. His closest friends were those he met at the Phoenix-area tracks. Most were White, some were Hispanic and a few were Black — who, in addition to that sole Black driver, worked on the racing crews.

Like most his age, Kyle was big on social media, but he only used it for what he could find about other racers and cars. He would research racers' backgrounds to see what they used for inspiration. He would also try to find what he could on cars, everything from motors to safety systems.

Kyle specifically would *not* use social media to gossip or put down others. His elders and parents had no online presence, so neither would he share about birthdays, weddings or other family issues, as many do.

Some drivers would show up for street racing in Glendale, an activity Kyle avoided. Though at first it sounded fun, he knew street racing was both illegal and dangerous. His elders taught him not to break laws, even the White man's laws. Better to focus on what was right than on what was fun. Illegal street racing, in Kyle's view, was yet another distraction.

He knew social media offered a way of getting your name out there. The more he was known, the more likely he would be to find sponsors to pay for his racing equipment, and opportunities to advertise, like any sports star. As a Navajo coming from the reservation, he thought companies might want to give him a chance to serve as a role model.

Racing cars for a living is expensive. You have to have the car, a specialized engine, and a crew. Neither he nor most teenagers could afford these on their own.

Winning races doesn't depend on the type of car as much as much as it depends on the engine, key parts of the car and, of course, the driver's ability. Kyle chose an old Chevy Nova with a brand-new racing engine.

At the moment he was being sponsored by a company owned by Phillip Stevens, who treated him professionally and with respect. Kyle liked that. He knew that if he did well, both he and Stevens would make some money. The bigger the wins, the more the money. His social-media profile drew a lot of attention, and many young women numbered among his followers. While cautious about that, he was happy he had a following.

Stevens was among a group of fellow owners who started a diversity program for drivers. The idea was to bring more people of color and women into the industry. Kyle loved this, as it fit with what his parents always taught him about diversity and respect.

NASCAR too had a program for charities, which appealed to him greatly. While some were specific, such as helping children with cancer, there was leeway for drivers to help youth with any programs they liked.

Kyle had learned in high school to be charitable. He was with the Junior Reserve Officer Training Corps program at that time. They would give food to the needy at the holidays and go into nearby elementary schools to teach younger students how to read. Charity was important, and Kyle viewed it as his lifelong mission.

To most onlookers, racing is not typically linked with the environment. Moving at high speeds takes a lot of high-grade fuel. Kyle's classmates started talking to him about racing and its effect on global warming, and how they needed to do something positive for the environment to offset this.

Kyle brought these concerns to Stevens, who promptly installed solar panels at the track. But he let Kyle and his crew know that he wanted to do more.

Kyle's sister Vanessa came to inform him that Grandfather Tsinnie wanted to talk. Kyle knew that traditional elders did not make appointments for family. Rather, they would just stop by. It was extremely informal, a way of letting family know they were always accepted and welcomed with encouragement. He could stop by his grandfather's modern manufactured home or come see him at the hogan, also close by. It didn't matter which home he'd visit; he just enjoyed Grandpa's company and advice.

Kyle found him in the hogan.

"Son," Grandpa began. "I want you to carry on the traditions, and you know this. There are the old traditions like religion, language and culture. I know you know about this because we taught you for all the years you were growing up. I have faith that you will do all that, but there is another tradition: the Warrior way. The way of being a warrior is different than years ago. You no longer have to fight the White man's army. But you do have to stand up for what's right, whether it's the rights of your grandma or your mother, or other tribes, or the health of your people, or for Mother Earth. All these things are related.

"One war is the fight against uranium, cancer and pollution. Hundreds of polluted uranium mines remain open on the Navajo Nation, many near Tuba City. The federal government was supposed to clean them up, but that will cost hundreds of millions of dollars, so many remain. Among our people this has been known to cause cancer. Many have died painful deaths. You must do what you can to have the federal government address this issue. Our tribal government doesn't have enough money for basic programs now and can't do much financially, but they must have a say in how and when this is addressed."

"I've heard about this, but I don't know much about it," Kyle said. "I will look into it and see what I can do. I'll get the community involved. I'll speak out about this when I give public talks."

Grandpa had few teeth, but was able to break through with a smile, letting Kyle know he was happy with his response. Grandpa also raised his hand and gave the OK sign. He then hugged his grandson.

Kyle left his meeting with Grandpa thinking about uranium, but even more about his upcoming race.

***

Saturday: race time.

Like all the other drivers, Kyle wore a helmet, pads, and had all kinds of safety devices on him and on his car. All are well aware that racing at speeds exceeding 200 miles per hour is always risky and carries with it certain dangers.

Yet despite all the safety measures, drivers periodically are injured and sometimes (though rarely) even killed in crashes.

On this day the race began in overcast weather. It didn't take long for things to go south. The first two laps proceeded as usual, with most of the cars close together. On the third lap, one of another driver's wheels touched Kyle's — never a good thing at such high speed. The other vehicles were able to get out of their way, so a pileup was avoided.

The other car spun out to the left and came to rest on that side of the track. Kyle's car went to the right, but his car hit hard into the wall before it stopped. This was nothing life-threatening, but he felt a deep pain in his right foot and leg — his driving foot, so it concerned him right away. Kyle's pit crew immediately called the ambulance.

This was not a good feeling. He didn't know how serious the setback, nor how long this would last. The hospital staff took X-rays, gave him pain pills, and told him the doctor would meet with him in the morning.

***

Dr. Anthony DiSalvo told him the injury was not permanent. He would keep him one more day, to keep an eye on his leg and foot, but Kyle would need just a few days' rest and then would be back to normal if there were no complications.

Kyle's father Daniel walked into his son's room.

"Grandpa called to say that the Native American Environmental Conference will be held at the Drury Inn in Flagstaff this weekend — and that this would be a good chance for you to talk to other environmentalists about the uranium situation on Navajo. It would be good for you to go. Besides, Sherman Alexie will be there signing his books. That's one of the reasons I want to go."

"I've always wanted to meet Alexie," Kyle responded. "Cool. I'll talk to people about the uranium issue too."

"We'll make it fun. I'll see if Grandpa is up to going."

"Looking forward to it. I'll drive my Nova because it'll bring more attention to my driving and maybe we can get more sponsors." Kyle flashed a smile to his dad.

"Okay, but don't forget the reasons we're there. The uranium, the environment and maybe some cultural lessons from Alexie. Don't get distracted."

"I won't. I just want to add to the conversation and have fun with it."

"That's fine."

***

On Saturday morning Kyle drove the souped-up Chevy, his dad and grandpa accompanying him on their way from Tuba City to Flagstaff.

"This is good," his father said. "Three generations together, trying to save Mother Earth."

Kyle grinned and Grandpa gave a thumbs up.

Kyle was used to hotels from all his travels, and Daniel had also seen his share, but Grandpa rarely left the rez and had only seen hotels that were one or two stories — not the ten-story monstrosity that overlooked NAU. They walked through the main lobby to the elevator.

"I've heard of elevators. I hope they're reliable," Grandpa said as Kyle pushed the button.

They stepped off into the conference center on the third floor and were invited to register. Aside from this table, twenty or more vendor tables were set up for attendees to pass by on their way to the main room for the speakers.

Sherman Alexie had the largest table, in the center of the line. His books were prominently displayed for sale. There were more copies of *Smoke Signals* than any of the others.

The trio started eyeing all the tables as they waited to register. Most attracted only two or three people; Alexie's table had at least twenty waiting in line.

"Let's go see Sherman Alexie. I want him to sign my book," Kyle urged.

As the three stood in line, Daniel asked Kyle to hold their place while he took Grandpa over to the Starbucks further down the hallway.

"That's fine. I know Grandpa wants his iced coffee. Can you get me a white chocolate mocha?"

The father nodded as the two started down the hall.

A Nativeteen with a *Don't Worry, Be Hopi* tee shirt took his place in line behind Kyle. Kyle let him know he was holding places for two others.

"I get that. I'm Allen," the teen said.

"I'm Kyle. I'm from Navajo."

Allen tried to make friendly small talk; he didn't find it easy to make new friends.

"I'm looking forward to meeting Alexie Sherman," Allen started awkwardly.

"What's up with that?" Kyle snapped. "It's Sherman Alexie, not Alexie Sherman."

Allen was embarrassed but also taken aback by Kyle's belligerent response.

"I don't know why I said that," he muttered. "I know better."

Allen looked away from Kyle, afraid the situation would get more heated. As he did, he couldn't help but notice a young Native woman walking by in tight jeans and shirt.

"Now you're staring at that woman's ass!" Kyle accused, giving Allen a dirty look. "Don't you have any respect?"

"I was just looking in the other direction. Why are you so judgmental?"

"You weren't just looking in the other direction — you were ogling her butt."

"Who died and made you chief?"

"You need to grow up!"

The two were growing more agitated by the second, both raising their voices. Flagstaff Police Officer Scott May arrived unnoticed, as the two were too busy yelling. "You two need to settle down. I really don't want to arrest both of you for disorderly conduct. So, whatever your problem is, work it out or take it elsewhere. Can you guys do that?"

Both nodded. Neither wanted to go to jail.

"No more trouble or I will haul you both in. Do you understand?"

Again, they nodded. As soon as the officer left, Kyle glared at the Hopi teen.

"We need to take this outside," Kyle said.

"We can do that."

Avoiding the elevator, they took the stairs to the lobby and went out the back door.

Not more than a minute outside and before a single punch was thrown, the boys heard that distinctive popping sound of live rounds being fired inside the hotel. It didn't last long, maybe thirty seconds. Soon police and ambulance arrived, sirens screaming, from all directions toward the scene.

"W-what th' hell?" Allen sputtered.

"We'd better get in there." Kyle grabbed the teen.

They ran back into the hotel and saw people in the lobby dropped to the floor.

"Stay where you are!" a security guard bellowed. "The shots came from up above, but we don't know if it's safe to go up there."

Kyle then realized that he got so caught up in the fight that he forgot about holding his father and grandfather's place in line and where they were. They had gone off. What floor were the shots coming from? He was suddenly frightened for their safety. He started shaking.

"Are you okay?" Allan asked.

"My father and grandpa are up there. I need to find out if they're okay. Was anybody with you?

"No, I came alone. But we need to see how your father and grandfather are doing."

At that point heavily armed police entered, guns drawn. EMTs hung back, ready to attend to any injured when it was safe.

The lead officer told those in the lobby to go wait outside.

The police officers started up the stairs while other officers guarded the elevator. Police then secured the hotel's perimeter as a unit made its way inside.

In twos and threes, people began to emerge from the building with officers guiding them to a safe area. Then a dozen victims were taken away in ambulances, many with gunshot wounds but some with other injuries, such as from shattered glass.

***

Kyle spotted his father being wheeled out in a gurney. He ran over.

"Dad, dad!"

"I'm okay, just a flesh wound and cuts from what I can tell but — your grandpa is gone."

"What do you mean *gone?*"

"I mean he was shot and killed."

Kyle went numb.

Allen, close by, had been watching the entire event unfold. He stood silent as father and son broke down, not knowing quite what to do.

Kyle hung onto the gurney as the EMT placed Daniel in the waiting ambulance.

"Is there any way I can help? Allen offered.

"No, but thank you for that. I'll go with him to the hospital."

"Good luck. I'll pray for you and your relatives."

"I appreciate that. Thank you again."

***

Daniel was released three days later. Kyle had stayed by his father's side for most of that time, leaving only to update his family.

Daniel said the shooting happened so fast that most security guards weren't able to respond in time. One policeman, Officer May, was able to bring down the gunman, shooting and killing the deranged man. So senseless. In addition to Grandpa, four others were killed and a dozen more injured. Lives changed forever.

Daniel was able to compose himself long enough to tell Kyle that his grandpa wanted more than anything else for them to carry on the family culture and work toward the common good of their people. That meant staying active in their community and focusing especially on the uranium mines. He emphasized too that Grandpa wanted him to follow his heart.

The funeral was planned for the following week. On returning to Tuba City, the family gathered at Grandpa's old hogan to show respect to him and discuss how to pay for the funeral. The $10,000 cost would be difficult to cover. Kyle could contribute a few thousand from his racing funds, but it would take him longer to come up with more. Most could only contribute a couple of hundred.

During their meeting, the phone rang and the display showed the funeral home, so Kyle picked up. The funeral director informed him that an anonymous benefactor had paid their funeral costs.

"But who?" Kyle insisted on knowing.

"As I said, he wishes to remain anonymous. I never got a name, phone number or address," the funeral director said. "All I can tell you is that it was a young Native American man."

***

When the postponed conference reconvened at the Coconino Center, there were three parts to it. The first dealt with the uranium-mining issue, the second was devoted to solar energy, and the third was a speech about poaching in Africa.

During the mining discussion some elders spoke about the cancers and other health problems believed to be related to the uranium mines, and how many of those sites had not been cleaned up. They agreed to contact their state's congressional members and others who might fund the cleanup of the mines. There was talk of hiring lawyers and potential litigation, but they weren't sure how to proceed or even whether they could afford it.

The second part, about solar energy, featured speakers from the industry and nonprofits about the benefits of moving away from fossil fuels.

One clear benefit is that you are helping Mother Earth. Another is that you aren't connected to the grid, so you become more self-sufficient. Most meeting attendees were interested in solar, but wanted to know more about how it worked and how much it would cost. So, company representatives agreed to meet with those families at their homes to show how solar could help them, since the impacts are different based on size and other variables.

The third part of the meeting captured most of Kyle's interest as a professor of ecology from Prescott College began showing slides from Africa. Impressed by the landscape and exotic animals,

Kyle was most taken by the African culture, noting cultural and other similarities between Native Americans and Africans.

Then his mind went from beauty to shock at the images of poached rhinos, elephants and other large creatures. The professor, Andrew Walden, also showed the sadness, in slide after slide, of tribal people and environmentalists overtaken by grief caused by these brutal assaults. These African tribes, Kyle learned, had to hire their own security to protect the wildlife — an expensive and ongoing battle.

Kyle thought about his elders, how they taught him to love all living beings.

He had to join the fight in this faraway land. He wondered if there were any racetracks in Africa — and if there weren't, could he start one?

6

Massimo Ferrara

Massimo Ferrara was different from other seventeen-year-olds in Hackensack, New Jersey, because his father was a jeweler.

And not your typical jeweler. Most jewelers either buy the jewelry ready-made or purchase the stones from retailers. Then they either assemble the piece or sell it for a markup as they received it. Many jewelers never leave their stores (or the cities they work in), as everything is delivered.

Though Massimo's father Rayford loved the business, he was a bit of a purist and adventurer: a purist in the sense that he wanted to find the gems himself and create something uniquely his, an adventurer in that he would go to exotic places to find them. His gem-finding missions took him to Africa four times a year, to various countries, for one or two weeks at a time.

For rubies he would go to Mozambique. For a gem known as tanzanite he would visit Tanzania. For emeralds he went to Zambia, more specifically down the Kafubu River. For gold, South Africa, and for diamonds, Zimbabwe, Angola, Liberia, Sierra Leone and Congo.

While his primary focus was on jewelry, Ray didn't limit his knowledge to that. Whenever he planned to travel to an African country, he would research it before he left. He wanted to know about its economics, whether it was safe to travel there, whether he would be permitted to travel with gems, facts about the culture, and how he could best communicate and get along with the people.

Massimo knew this to be his family's way of life, where his father would be gone four times a year and come home with wonderful gems, stories, and photos. These were of African people, their art, their environment and astonishing wildlife.

The stories and photos were mesmerizing. They captivated Massimo and made him want to go to Africa. He would often tell his friends, but they were more interested in their social circles. How many teenagers, after all, even think about going to Africa?

This led to an interest that developed into a passion. Geography, international politics and earth science became important areas of study. He saw some who had no interest in school, others who were only interested in getting good grades, but nobody like him, motivated to learn more — about *Africa*. For a White kid growing up in New Jersey, this was unusual.

Massimo knew that going there would require a lot of preliminary work. He would have to study its countries as his father did. He would need to be physically fit as well. He would have to know map-reading and route-finding. He would have to know first aid if he or someone else was injured. He would have to raise money.

Above all this new excitement revived an old fascination with nature in him. Massimo scanned the internet for environmental groups, hiking groups, and anything he could learn about New Jersey's parks and wildlife. He found two designated wilderness areas: Brigantine Wilderness, 11 miles north of Atlantic City; and Great Swamp National Refuge in Morris County.

Massimo always loved nature. As a child he would go down to the creek in back of his elementary school and catch frogs. He and his mother reached an agreement: he could bring frogs home as long as he kept them in the garage. Neither was entirely happy, but both could live with it. His father would shrug and steer clear of any arguing, but he was careful not to run over any frogs with his car.

It would drive Massimo's mother nuts. She would come home, open the garage door and find giant bullfrogs hopping all over the garage. Massimo would let them go every five days and return them to the creek. Then he would bring in a new batch.

Though Massimo wanted to follow in his father's footsteps, he wasn't sure about being a jeweler. But he was wild about someday going to Africa. He wanted to experience Africa with the stories, culture, environment and wildlife the way his father did.

After his dad got home from one of his African trips, Massimo couldn't wait to hear his stories and see the photos.

Ray was wiry but in shape. Though his trips were only about four times a year, he had to be ready. On evenings and weekends, starting from when Massimo was little, his dad would go on hikes and take the boy with him.

By the time Massimo was a teenager he would go off by himself or with friends from school on local hikes. His dad, his teachers and other adults frequently told him that it wasn't safe to go hiking alone, but if he couldn't find anybody, off he went anyway.

Ray taught him the science of putting together a backpack, especially the importance of water and a small first-aid kit. The exact amounts of supplies, he learned, depended on how far he was going and whether the hike was strenuous. Without enough water and food, hiking can be dangerous. With too much, the backpack can be too heavy to carry and slow him down.

Two of his favorite trails were the Ramapo Park and Cannonball Trail and the Ramapo Reservation Trail. The Ramapo Trail and Cannonball Trail is 5.4 miles long and goes by a lake. The Ramapo Reservation Trail is 7.2 miles, also goes by a lake, and is a bit harder. Massimo was always drawn to water because that meant more wildlife and flowers. He liked to photograph the butterflies and frogs. Then he would look them up online to identify their species.

One day he decided to try the Stairway to Heaven Trail just because of its name. Ray often listened to that song, and Massimo could play it in his head while he walked. He wouldn't listen to music on his hikes because that would take away from the sounds of nature — he wanted to hear the birds chirping and the amphibians.

He found the Stairway to Heaven Trail much more captivating than the song. It was only 2.9 miles, but a lot was packed into that: a boardwalk, a suspension bridge, a hardwood forest and plenty of flowers. The best part, though, was the waterfall.

Other people were on the trail, but not a lot, just enough to let him know they were there, in small enough groups that he could relax without hearing too much from them.

Massimo sat on a large boulder next to the beautiful waterfall and simply stared. He stared and lost track of time. It was so relaxing. After a while, he closed his eyes and listened to the sound of the falls and of birds nearby, soaking it all in. He felt so peaceful, he fell asleep.

***

Massimo opened his eyes, not sure whether he was dreaming.

A red-headed girl about his age was dancing on a tree branch hanging over the creek, humming a tune. She couldn't have been more than five feet tall and if she weighed over ninety it would have been a surprise. Her petiteness made her agile, and she used that to dance all over the tree limb.

Massimo thought she moved like Huck Finn, but she was even more impressive. Huck just balanced himself while walking across fences; she danced across the branch. She would curl her feet around the limb so that she was actually on the side of it. She was, in fact, sideways. How or why, she didn't fall off was amazing.

Massimo couldn't help himself, he had to say something. "Hey! You're going to hurt yourself!" he yelled.

The girl looked at him and smiled. "I don't hurt myself often."

"You've done this before?"

"Many times, and I've only broken my legs twice. They heal quickly," she said matter-of-factly.

"What are those dance moves, anyway?" Massimo asked, still taken aback.

"They're mostly from the old movie where Fred Astaire was dancing on the ceiling. I'm still not able to dance upside down on the branch, but at least I've been able to curl my feet so I can dance sideways."

By this time, Massimo was bordering on speechless. His eyes kind of rolled around. "I never heard of Fred Astaire or that movie."

"I've been interested in dance for a long time, so I researched it, and my parents used to watch it. It's from way back, but I think it's the cat's meow," she said.

"You could seriously hurt yourself."

"Like they say, no pain, no gain."

***

He introduced himself, but remained a little tongue-tied; to him, her beauty was like finding nature in nature.

"I'm Janet McMurty," she said.

Massimo's senses started to return, along with his sense of humor. "Good to know you, and I hope you live long enough for me to know you better."

"It's safer than you think. I've practiced it so many times," she said.

Janet didn't want to linger on the dangers, so she changed the subject. "What's your favorite bird?"

The question caught him off guard. "I haven't thought about it much. I like birds, but I'm more of a frog guy," he replied.

"What types of frogs?"

"Any type, but the bullfrogs seem the most prevalent around here." Massimo thought. "I do have one favorite bird. It's the pileated woodpecker. I just love woodpeckers and the way they peck away. But this one is special. It pecks slower than other kinds, and makes a shrieking sound that sorta sounds like laughter. It's just fun to watch."

"Do you like wildlife?"

"Very much."

"I go on hikes a lot so I see a lot of wildlife," Janet mused. "I've seen raccoons and snakes on this trail, but in my other places I've seen bears walking through the woods, bobcats sunning — I damn near walked into a bobcat one time."

Massimo thought this was too good to be true. A beautiful girl in a beautiful place. *How does it get any better than this?*

"Do you always keep your thoughts to yourself?" Janet asked.

"No. You just caught me at an odd moment," he responded. "I like most of the same things you just talked about. Tell me about yourself."

***

Janet was seventeen too. She talked about her high school and parents, who were teachers, and how their mutual love of teaching made them a natural match. Massimo wondered if Janet and his mutual love of nature made *them* a natural match.

After hours of talking and losing track of time, Janet asked Massimo if he would like to see Buttermilk Falls.

"What's that?" he asked.

She described a ninety-foot waterfall — the largest in New Jersey — and among the highest in the states along the East Coast.

The Buttermilk Falls Trail is 7.2 miles and steep, she told him, but well worth the trek to see this majestic cataract.

So, true to his wish, their love of nature and waterfalls in particular brought them together. Eager to make a plan, Massimo researched the waterfalls of New Jersey. He found a website showing the twelve hidden waterfalls. He was ecstatic, hoping this could mean a dozen more days of adventure with Janet, assuming he could talk her into accompanying him.

Next, he looked up the state's best hikes and found Mt. Tammany, Giant Stairs and South Mountain Hemlock Falls. More nature and more Janet were the plan. He would tell her about the waterfalls and best hikes.

Massimo thought to look up local wildlife too, and was astounded to find that New Jersey has 134 varieties of freshwater fish and 336 different marine fish. The wildlife includes wild turkey, peregrine falcon, eagles, osprey, beavers, coyote, grouse and fox. The teens made sure to keep an eye out for them during their adventures.

Before Massimo met Janet, he would keep to himself; apart from a handful of friends he'd see from time to time, he didn't socialize much. But with Janet he felt they should go out more. He knew she liked that. Sometimes they would just hang or have drinks or play video games with their friends.

***

The two started spending their evenings with other teenagers at Tom's Lake, a few blocks from Massimo's house. The lake officially closed at sundown, which is precisely when the teenagers would start showing up.

It began for the most part innocently, with swimming and passing around a few beers, maybe a joint or two. As time went on, some in the group started skinny-dipping.

Within weeks *all* the teenagers took to skinny-dipping, nearly thirty of them. No one in the community seemed to catch on. This continued for at least two months. The teens were having the time of their lives, exposed, unreserved, unabashed in their enjoyment.

One night, well after dark, police spotlights came on and the cops rushed in, nabbing and arresting as many skinny-dippers as they could. Spotting her chance, Janet, naked, took off into the woods, avoiding detection by hiding in a log. Massimo and most of the others weren't so lucky. The police carted them away.

Massimo's parents weren't happy. The boy pled guilty, but this wasn't a felony charge and the judge sentenced him to community service. This meant picking up trash at Tom's Lake, which suited him, because he hated trash and would pick it up anyway, so it wasn't much of a punishment.

He went one step further and asked Janet and his friends to join him. To love nature, after all, means that one must work to keep it as pristine as possible.

Massimo expressed this to the judge along with his plans for the wider cleanup. Judge Josh Robertson smiled and told Massimo he knew one of the local Sierra Club leaders and would connect the two so they could have a big cleanup day.

"I don't see why not," the judge added.

Massimo had already worked with the Sierra Club and its cleanup projects, picking up trash near waterfalls and streams. For him this would be a lifelong commitment, as he would see beautiful areas and wish to help keep them clean. The plastic containers that people left behind, he knew, hurt the birds, as they often get their heads caught in them. Cigarette butts too are an environmental hazard: they can start fires.

Massimo also attended Sierra Club online lectures and talked with club members, friends, classmates and teachers about global warming.

Of course, he would talk with Janet too. When it came to the environment, his passion became infectious. They talked constantly, for hours, and got more and more insight about land and the protection it needs as they hiked together.

Apart from issues that touched on the environment, Massimo would avoid any talk about politics. When Sierra Club members brought it up, specifically with regard to the importance of elections, Massimo would tune them out.

***

Mark Stewart, a visiting political-science professor at William Paterson College, had a speech coming up about Africa. This was something Massimo felt he couldn't miss — with Janet by his side, of course.

Stewart had been to most of the countries in Africa to learn about their politics, and spoke about widespread discontent, rampant use of teen soldiers, sex trafficking and dictatorships.

Yet he spoke too of the beauty of Africa: its great forests, rivers and waterfalls. He spoke about the vastness of Congo River.

He talked about Africa's unique mountains, deserts, big wildlife, enormous trees and exotic flowers. He contrasted its ugliness with its stunning beauty. Then came his talk about poachers.

With tears, he evoked the gentleness of elephants, and wondered aloud, *how could poachers do what they do?* even though he well knew why.

Smitten and devastated at the same time, Massimo made his mind up to go to Africa. It wasn't a question of whether, but when.

The only remaining question was, could he talk Janet into going?

7

Lizzy Feinstein

Lizzy Feinstein was happy with her life growing up in Seattle, but during high school she made some bad decisions.

She was smart, getting good grades in tough subjects when other kids couldn't. But during her sophomore year Lizzy hooked up with the wrong boy. Several girls at her school did this; they would date boys far below their intelligence or standing.

The teachers, counselors and parents who noticed could neither understand nor, it appeared, do anything about it.

Lizzy repeated the mistake four times in four years with the same guy, resulting in four children. Every time the guy would screw up and she would send him packing, back he'd be, having sworn he'd changed his ways. Her parents and friends implored her to reconsider her choice to let him back into her life, yet she wouldn't listen. "But I love him," she'd say.

After four years and more frustration than she could stand, Lizzy realized the relationship wasn't working, life had become too hard and she told the guy she was done with him — and this time she meant it.

Not only wouldn't he help pay the bills, he seemed invisible as far as paying attention to her or the kids. He may have been present physically, but in terms of helping he was a ghost and she considered him nameless.

Four years and four kids later, Lizzy saw her error, but too late. Her dreams of becoming a lawyer were gone. It was all she could do to get through her day — financially, physically and mentally — for her kids.

***

Lizzy had not gone to synagogue for years. Both her parents were Jewish, one conservative and somewhat religious, the other nonpracticing. She grew up knowing the basics of Judaism, learned much about the Holocaust, knew the Friday night prayers over wine and bread, but not much else. Some people referred to her as a *cultural Jew*. She loved lox and bagels but felt ignorant of the history and traditions.

Frustrated, Lizzy started going back to synagogue. She wasn't looking for salvation; rather, she was hoping to find some sense out of life and try to keep her sanity.

The members of her synagogue were diverse. Some were conservative politically, and some were liberal. Some liked modern music, some liked Lawrence Welk. Some dressed in finery for the religious services yet did not look down on the poor in their community, who would arrive in whatever they could manage to cobble together.

The part she liked best about her synagogue was that every Sunday they would give food boxes to the poor. They did what they could to help the community. They didn't ask the people who showed up for food whether they were Jewish or belonged to some other religion.

One Sunday Lizzy showed up to help put the food boxes together and hand them out. This is where she met Ben Shain. Ben had a nice personality. Never the kind of person who yells, and neither did he suffer fools.

"Don't say stupid stuff," he would tell people, whenever they said things that didn't make sense. He was particularly annoyed with people who believed anything they read on the internet and had even less patience with conspiracy theorists.

Lizzy took a liking to Ben. Ben liked Lizzy too. They had the synagogue in common. They were both kindhearted and liked to help deliver food to the poor. They wanted to help others as much as they could. Yet with four kids, Lizzy's time and energy was limited. She could only help out for a few hours on Sunday because that was the only time her cousin could watch her kids.

Ben was assistant director of the City of Seattle's transportation program, so he was in on official discussions about what the city could do to help the environment, especially around issues related to climate change.

For Ben's department, this meant developing more programs for public transportation and providing support for electric vehicles, such as allocating more spaces for people to energize their car batteries. City officials and transportation planners were concerned about air pollution and air quality.

Ben attended other meetings as well about what the various departments were doing about climate change and the environment. All city departments were recycling whatever they could. Housing offered incentives to businesses and homebuilders to use solar or wind to cut down on use of fossil fuels and become more energy-efficient. Homelessness too, particularly among veterans, was a growing problem with no easy solution. The city was doing what it could to help.

Another area of concern to Ben involved polluted waters, especially the high incidence of illegal dumping, and how it was making some of the waters rancid and killing fish in large numbers.

In particular, he saw problems with algae — from the pollution — that was turning the water strange colors. Clean air and clean water were issues near and dear to him.

Ben loved the outdoors and would ask Lizzy to go walking with him, but she could rarely get much time away. She liked the idea, and was curious about hiking, which she hadn't done. It took her a couple of months, but she managed to work out a schedule with relatives to watch the kids so she could try it.

They would start by going on small walks in the parks near her house. Then they started going to Seattle's better-known parks, including Discovery Park, Green Lake Park and Myrtle Edwards Park.

"So, this is what hiking is like?" she asked on one of the easy walks with Ben.

Knowing she knew little about hiking, he offered suggestions about appropriate footwear. (Lizzy didn't know what hiking boots were or even that they existed when they started going on walks.) He told her that her sneakers were okay for the short walks, but that for more serious nature trails, she would need some hiking boots.

"The boots need to be snug, but not too tight. If too loose, you can get blisters," Ben warned.

He would talk to her about the beautiful trails he would go on by himself or with a local hiking club. She was interested — in him, in nature, and being able to get a break from her kids.

Ben showed Lizzy how to find certain trails online to learn the lengths and how hard they were to do, and view photos to decide how enticing they were.

Ben would let Lizzy choose the trail, that way she could find out for herself what she was capable of doing. After a while, as he began to learn her limits, he would help her pick trails that she could do.

They started on some of the better-known trails in the Seattle area that weren't too hard: Ebey's Landing, Mt. Pilchuck and Rattlesnake Ledge.

Anything with 'rattlesnake' in the name was a problem. Lizzy didn't like snakes. Ben convinced her, though, that as long as she stayed on the trail and kept her eyes peeled, there wouldn't be any problems with snakes or any other critters she didn't like.

Her nails were another potential problem. Not having much money, Lizzy spent most of what she earned on her kids; yet once in a blue moon she would treat herself and get her nails done. Out on these hikes, she always worried that if she fell, she'd break her lovely long green nails.

"We'll try not to let that happen," Ben assured her, knowing it could happen at any moment.

***

While Ben loved to see Lizzy as much as he could, he understood her time was limited. On those days when she couldn't come on walks, he would go on hikes with Emerald City Wanderers, a Seattle hiking club.

Ben didn't mind hiking alone, but Lizzy and his parents would tell him repeatedly that doing so could be dangerous. While he would hike alone occasionally, Ben liked the inclusiveness of the hiking club with its broad age range and diversity, and he soon made friends with many of the hikers.

Diversity and inclusion were important to Lizzy too. It was part of what made living in Seattle great: so many different people all mixed together, different races, different religions, different lifestyles.

His love for diversity was one more reason Lizzy enjoyed hanging out with Ben. She very much liked him but, still feeling burned, she didn't want anything serious. With four kids, thoughts of sex were pushed to the back of her mind, and she certainly didn't want any more children.

"Good God! I can't imagine having more kids," she told Ben without being asked.

If she could have an adult friend, though, who liked to go on hikes and with whom she could have fun, well, why not?

Having done many (if not most) of the local hikes, both wanted more. Ben found a book on national parks and together they started exploring the options, starting with the national parks in their state.

The closest one to Seattle was Mount Rainier National Park.

"So, let's start there," Lizzy said.

She'd read up about the place. According to her book, the park had the best and most wildflowers of any national park in the country, beautiful waterfalls and mountain streams that seemingly went on forever, glorious mountains rising over 14,000 feet, as well as the old growth forest. Its history also bore the stamp of Native American culture.

"I have to go. *We* have to go," she blurted out.

Ben laughed and said he felt the same way.

"It's just a matter of planning and working out the details," he said.

This was no small endeavor. Ben had to make arrangements to take off from work. Lizzy had to find someone she could trust to watch her kids. Both would need to know for how long they would be gone, how much money they would need, what vehicle would be required, how much food to bring along and what they would take in their packs on the trails.

They also had to figure out sleeping arrangements, which felt awkward all around. Neither one wanted to bring it up. Ben couldn't be sure what Lizzy wanted. Lizzy was afraid to tell Ben she didn't yet want sex — and anxious he might call off the trip should she bring it up.

"I know what to do," Ben said. "I'll call the Sierra Club. They have people who lead hikes there and can give us advice on every detail."

They had gone on day hikes together but had never done overnights. Would they camp out — and if so, in tents for one, or for two? Would they get rooms at the nearby lodges? One room or two?

These questions weighed on their minds, but neither wanted to start the conversation. Each looked at the other awkwardly. Ben would go with the flow; but Lizzy, after some thought, felt she had to make her position clear up front.

"I'm not ready to have sex yet," she informed him. "I needed to tell you that."

Ben smiled because he already knew.

"You said *yet*," he replied. "I understand."

They decided on a two-person tent. It was easier to set up than separate tents, and more convenient since they planned to camp out for two nights. They wanted to spend as much time there as possible, but didn't want to pressure themselves too much. A three-day trip seemed perfect. They counted the days till they could go.

Their contact from the Sierra Club would meet them at Mt. Rainier to lead them on at least one hike and help accustom them to the park.

On arriving at the Paradise Inn Welcome Center, Ben and Lizzy spotted Bryce, the guide from the Sierra Club, waiting for them. Ben recognized him immediately from his website photo: a big burly mustache and Indiana Jones–style fedora.

Before they could introduce themselves, a little boy ran up to Bryce and asked him if he was a cowboy.

Bryce winced. "Well, er, no."

"But you're wearing a cowboy hat," the little boy said.

"Sorry, son, but it's not a cowboy hat. It's an Indiana Jones hat," he carefully pointed out.

"Whose Indiana Jones?" the boy wanted to know.

The generational divide was painfully clear.

"He was an adventurer in the movies — but ask your dad," Bryce advised.

"I will!" the boy exclaimed, and wandered off.

Lizzy had seen photos of Comet Falls in Robert and Martha Manning's book *Walks of a Lifetime in America's National Parks*. She was tantalized by the waterfalls so it didn't take much arm-twisting: they were able to get Bryce to agree to a Comet Falls hike that night. They went through an old-growth forest before crossing a stream, and after 2.5 miles, seeing Comet Falls, at 320 feet the tallest waterfall in the park.

They sat for a couple hours just eating snacks, taking in the falls, listening in rapture to the water cascade, watching the birds and enjoying each other. The five-mile round trip was well worth it. They were certainly in love with nature, and not far from falling in love themselves.

That night they settled into a campground in the park. Lizzy fried some hamburgers on the portable grill while Ben set up the tent. Lizzy felt comfortable with their arrangement.

Ben was true to his word, but nevertheless found it difficult to sleep in the same tent with the woman he found so attractive. He wanted the relationship to last, so any hope for the future demanded that he somehow clear his mind and get himself to sleep.

***

Along with detailed information about the trails, Bryce told Ben and Lizzy about an upcoming Sierra Club speakers' series. For him, he explained, one stood out. It was easier, he found, for new folks presented with a roster of events to focus at first on just one.

He suggested a talk being given by Rhonda Jirak. She was with the Bullitt Foundation, an organization devoted to protecting and restoring the environment of the Pacific Northwest, and concerned, among other things, with global warming.

That sounded interesting. Ben and Lizzy told Bryce they would go.

On their second day, they decided to do as many miles as they could on the 93-mile Wonderland Trail. They planned to do thirteen, six and a half miles in and back.

They would walk at their own pace, stop for photos whenever they wanted and just enjoy themselves. This hike was great, and included several river crossings.

That night they were very happy. They enjoyed the waterfalls, the flowers, the streams, the rivers, the mountains and each other.

"The whole thing — all of it," Lizzy said when she affirmed to Ben how much she'd enjoyed the two days.

After dinner at the campground, they sat by the fire, drinking cheap wine and relaxing in each other's company.

They didn't want the night to end, but at last they grew tired and went into the tent and snuggled into their sleeping bags. Ben was drifting off. Lizzy, though, lay awake, staring into the darkness.

"Alone is no fun," she said aloud and slipped into Ben's sleeping bag with him.

He was already fast asleep. She snuggled up to him and looked up at the stars one more time before she too drifted off.

***

About two weeks after their trip, the speech on global warming came up.

Rhonda Jirak had talked about the causes and impact of global warming. She spoke about how glaciers in Alaska were melting, how droughts had increased throughout America as well as other countries. She talked about how extensive logging in Africa has caused less oxygen — and how these problems soon would become irreversible if not addressed now.

Rising temperatures — a direct result of global warming — means more droughts and more heat waves. Places such as Phoenix and other desert communities, which are already hot, will become unbearably so, causing more deaths, especially among the homeless.

An increase in the number and intensity of hurricanes, along with other changes in weather patterns, will adversely impact agriculture as well. That means considerably less fruit and vegetables.

Ice melting worldwide and rising sea levels will cause more floods. Global warming will also result in dirtier air. This will profoundly alter wildlife habitats.

Jirak said such changes are certain to wreak havoc on the economy, as homes, roads, bridges, railroad tracks and airport runways all will be in need of constant repair.

During the slideshow presentation, Lizzy was especially taken with Africa, by the contrast of beautiful pristine forests with those that had been logged and stricken bare.

"How could anybody do this?" Lizzy asked.

"Greed. Jobs. Money," Ben replied. "There is no question about the reasons, only the morality and the impact on people, the environment and the planet."

When Lizzy went home that night, she researched two things. First, global warming, to learn as much as she could about the issue; second, logging in Africa. She noticed that Congo had been deeply affected: where logging had not been done, there were beautiful waterfalls and streams and huge trees; where it *had* been done, the earth was denuded and water stopped flowing.

One reason why Congo popped up first on her internet search is that a Save the Forest group had been started in that country by some of its indigenous people. The more Lizzy read, the more her heart ached, but the Save the Forest group gave her hope.

Just as she had to go to Mount Rainier, she knew in that moment she had to go to Congo.

"I have to go — *we* have to go," she blurted out.

"This is sounding familiar," Ben said. "Where are we going this time?"

"Congo, in Africa," she answered.

Ben's eyes grew wide.

Lizzy told him all about what she found and how she felt.

"I was expecting you to come up with something else, but I didn't see this coming," Ben admitted. "But if you're going to do it, you can bet we're doing it together."

8

Meeting in Africa

Months passed by as Sky became more immersed in the Wantu people. They became his friends and extended family. He also joined the anti-poaching brigade as they fought to protect the wildlife as well as their own way of life. The Wantu stuck with calling him Sky rather than his recently recovered given name. It felt appropriate.

Sky had dissociative amnesia, a condition that results in a gap in memory, in which the person cannot remember important life events, especially those involving trauma or violence. Yet someone so afflicted may still remember daily routines and certain parts of his or her past.

The flower that Sky ate helped him recover most of his memory. He remembered he'd been in downtown Flagstaff when he encountered three men who at first seemed not to notice him but then glared as he passed by. Evidently this was a drug deal in progress. The three ran over to him and without saying a word started punching and kicking until he passed out.

When he came to, he was in an airplane. He didn't know what the drug dealers were planning, but he was sure it wasn't good. While growing up on Hopi, he took classes taught by a Korean martial-arts specialist who was married to a Hopi. His head ached and his ribs throbbed, but he knew he would have to do something quickly if he were going to survive.

Sky cautiously looked around and saw the men occupied with something else. No one was paying attention to him. This was good. He scanned the area, then looked above him: *parachutes*. He quickly found the exit door right under the chutes.

He'd been caught by surprise in the alley, but this time the element of surprise was on his side. His martial-arts training helped. He looked at the parachute. It seemed simple enough: tie on the strap and push the button when you needed to open it. Hopefully it would work.

Sky jumped up, grabbed the parachute and punched the man nearest to him, knocking him cold. The other hoodlums were too far back in the plane to react in time. He secured the parachute, tied it tight, yanked open the door and jumped.

His landing was not a good one — the trees were so dense in the forest coming up that he could not avoid running into them. Sky hit one tree, then ricocheted off another. Though the branches badly bruised and scraped him, they also broke his fall;

he just as easily could have broken his neck. As it was, he ended up hitting his head and for the second time was knocked out.

***

Sky knew that eventually he would have to go back home — he'd *want* to go back, to be with his people. But how could he leave his friends here behind forever? The question reminded him of some of his people, who lived in communities off the reservation because that's where they could find jobs.

Some of his friends were living in border towns close to home, others were farther away in Phoenix, still others in DC or California; what mattered was the quality and length of the visits back home, so they could participate in cultural and social events. That they practiced their culture as much as they could was always important to his people.

So now the question was, how often would he walk between the worlds of Hopi and Wantu? He had walked in two worlds before, the Hopi and White man's worlds, navigating the world of differences in the cultures.

The Navajo reservation surrounds the Hopi reservation, and Sky had many Navajo friends. He found that for the most part, Navajos and Hopis got along. Many Navajos worked in Hopi communities and vice versa, with a considerable amount of inter-marriage, as with his Navajo father and Hopi mother. Years back, land issues between the two tribes caused frequent conflict, but much of that was settled or at least greatly diminished as the Navajos and Hopis found common ground.

As for the Wantu, as much as that tribe was self-sufficient, they still periodically had to go into the closest town of Wassabe for supplies. Sky had not yet been there, so he asked Joseph if he could go to see what it was like.

***

As soon as the sun rose over the horizon, a contingent of seven Wantu and Sky started out for Wassabe, a three-hour drive and one of the most enjoyable and scenic that Sky had ever experienced. The forests were among the greenest on the planet, the perfect setting for birds of every color, some bright red, others bright yellow and bright green to go along with the variety of astonishing wildlife. They passed giraffes, zebras, rhinos and more. A sight to behold. Surreal.

Arriving in Wassabe, Sky thought it looked like an old country town. Not much here but a gas station, a grocery store, a motel and, oddly, a large building for community meetings. Odd because Wassabe contained little housing, just enough for the workers at the gas pump, store and motel. Yet it remained the closest town with groceries and other necessary supplies for the several hundred people who lived within the same range as the Wantu.

In the grocery store, Sky looked at the bulletin board of community events, one of which advertised Professor Walden for the following week. He would be discussing his most recent book about wildlife, poaching and Africa.

"Oh, I want to go!" Sky declared.

Joseph responded that he too wanted to hear what Walden had to say, and so he arranged the outing for the professor's presentation.

***

PoRue Kazzie knew that going to Africa required not only money, but time and planning as well. She'd saved thousands of her earnings from her job at the Navajo Zoo, doing whatever it took to fulfill her promise to herself that she would go to Africa and join in the fight against poaching.

It wasn't an easy commitment — one reason Kristal and Millie didn't plan to go with her. Kristal was committed to Special Olympics and becoming a special-education teacher; Millie was committed to social justice and starting her prelaw college work. Each felt drawn to her own special cause, involving specific requirements.

So, after graduation the three friends agreed to go their separate ways but stay in touch by social media and phone. They'd heard too many sad stories from their parents about how they lost touch with their friends over the years. Families and jobs became their primary focus and friendships slowly faded away. This trio was committed to not let that happen.

PoRue had been in touch with Dr. Walden. He'd compiled a contingent of college-age students to join him on the African tour to promote and highlight issues presented in his book and, most especially, to fight poaching. His reason for bringing students along was twofold.

First, the students could help with everything from loading equipment to documenting the trip and the manifold problems caused by poaching. Second, the professor had reached an age where he realized he wasn't going to live forever and became concerned about his legacy, particularly with regard to the prevention of poaching and the sustainability of wildlife and the environment. This was not only important, but one of the most noble causes. He wanted everyone involved, particularly the young people, to carry on this battle, to ensure that it would be ongoing.

***

Cynthia Baxter was another who joined the Walden team of teenagers committed to the cause — or rather, to finding out more about Africa and ways in which she might help.

Her experience with domestic violence gave her insight about the plight of battered women and an urge to try to improve their shattered lives. After what happened with her father that night when she called the police and fled, her whole world changed.

David was arrested, Susan moved out, got a restraining order against David, then filed for divorce. Cynthia talked with her mother often, but she kept communication with her dad to a bare minimum because of what he'd done over the years.

On the night of the arrest Cynthia went straight to the hospital to find Susan badly bruised and in need of stitches, but with no life-threatening injuries. The psychological part would be toughest for her mom. Cynthia decided to move in with Debbie, whose parents were understanding and agreed to let her stay with them until the trip to Congo.

She raised money by working in a domestic-violence shelter for women and children. Cynthia was good with battered women, sharing her background, what happened with her dad, and all that went on in her home. She would calm them with assurances that they could be safe, that they had choices, and to help them with their self-esteem, because she knew what they were going through, the toll that had been taken. She saw it firsthand, she would tell them, and knew the pattern. Working with these women opened Cynthia's eyes. She wanted to reach out, to help women with con-siderably less resources. Professor Walden talked of things she hadn't yet considered. Now, she wanted to learn more about how big a problem domestic violence was in Africa.

John, Debbie, Natasha and Zee were all concerned about the African problems too, but they wanted to work on the local prob-lems in northern Arizona, especially uranium mining and the ski-resort issue on the San Francisco Peaks. It seemed pretty clear that every year the entrepreneurs would come up with some way to make money that had a negative impact and imposed on Native Americans, the environment, or both.

Cynthia had a strong sense of what she needed to do. Her mom encouraged her to go on the African trip, and told her she was destined to do something great.

"If it's in Africa, then so be it," she said.

***

As for going to Africa, Kyle Tsinnie had the easiest time financially because his racing career had taken off.

Thanks to regular features in the *Navajo-Hopi Observer* and on KTNN radio, Kyle gained prominence and the kind of media attention that garnered him endorsements from companies making the sneakers and cars they advertised on the Navajo Nation and in casinos.

Though financially not a strain, the trip to Africa and joining in on the work involved a serious commitment from Kyle, as he well understood. It also meant leaving his father and other family members during his time there.

If his going into racing was novel, so too was this mission, a type of outreach to a people and community with which he had no prior experience. He would be one of few Native Americans who would travel to Africa to help prevent poaching, which for Kyle would involve a new and different set of skills.

It was hard for Walden to see precisely how a race-car driver fit into the poaching-prevention world, but when he met Kyle, he could readily see the young man's passion, not only for wildlife and protecting the environment, but for social justice as well. He saw too how effective Kyle could be, and how well he would relate to the Africans both in background and conversation.

***

Dr. Walden didn't much like the idea of taking teenage couples on his overseas trips; there was too much room for drama and problems. Most couples that age don't last very long, and a pair at war or shouting at each other was the last thing he wanted on this trip. Massimo and Janet, though, struck him as somehow different. Theirs was a shared passion — not only for each other but through that love, almost defining it, for their embrace of Africa. Neither had to debate with the other about going, Walden was sure.

***

When Ray first heard the words from Massimo's lips, he winced.

He thought his son had lost his mind. Anti-poaching? It took a lot of convincing on Massimo's part, over several months. He would talk to his dad every day about Africa, and show him photos. He would talk about Professor Walden and how safe the trip would be because he'd be in a group, as part of a team.

Yet, the jeweler knew the dangers only too well. He had many concerns, ranging from safety to career decisions that affected his son; but after a while, the thought occurred that perhaps this idea wasn't so crazy after all. Goals are personal. That he'd never encountered this one before made it no less significant for his son. It was perplexing to him, though, why or how Massimo came up with such a plan.

Having considered it, Ray concluded that if he didn't approve the Africa trip, his son would find a way to go there anyway, and that would cause a falling out. That would be intolerable. So, he proposed the idea that he would give his blessing — even help financially — if Massimo would agree to manage the store for at least a year when he returned.

"Wow — yes! I never thought I'd hear that from you," Massimo responded, shaking his father's hand.

Janet's parents were so busy with their nine other kids that they willingly let her go on the trip as long as she raised the money herself. Thanks to Massimo and his dad, she was able to do this by working hard at the jewelry store and managing her savings.

***

Going to Africa together as a pair was not in the cards for Ben Schain and Lizzy.

Ben had to remain where he was, to do his job with the City of Seattle. He would watch her kids, he promised, hiring a babysitter during his workday, if she agreed to go for no longer than a month.

So, the teens on Professor Walden's trip would tour different parts of Congo and Africa to learn the depth of the poaching problem.

***

Professor Walden gathered the group when they arrived at Newark Airport. PoRue, Cynthia, Kyle, Massimo and Janet, and Lizzy all piled into the meeting room.

"Greetings, and make yourselves at home," Walden told the group of environmentally friendly teenagers, then got right to the point. "As you are well aware by now, you will see not just some of the greatest beauty, but some of the ugliest devastation on earth, and sights and experiences for which there can be no real preparation. You will see wildlife tortured and killed for their horns. You may see people killed in their defense of poaching. The poachers are merciless, I must warn you. If any of you is having second thoughts — for any reason — I understand and will pay for your flight back home. But once you board that plane to Congo, you will be unable to leave till your time is up."

All understood and agreed.

***

Visiting each of the six tribes in Congo was eye-opening. Tribal officials showed the Walden team their elaborate security, including fences and guards to protect from the poachers.

Then the officials showed them the results of a breach: rhinos, elephants and other wildlife dead, killed for their horns by poachers. It was devastating for the teens to see this firsthand. Each appeared shaken to the core. They watched as tribal elders prayed over the dead. Their chins dropped in sorrow. Lizzy broke down and cried.

Each of their visits to these six tribes brought a similar mix of horror and consternation, eerie in the sense that nowhere did they see any actual poachers, only the hideous results of their work.

***

It came time to travel to Wassabe, where Walden was scheduled to speak. The event drew hundreds from nearby tribes, as many as would fit in the community center.

The professor talked with the people about the growing problems with poaching. Many were familiar with the trouble in their own areas, but had no idea how widespread the problem had become in other parts of the country and continent.

Walden spoke at length about the impact poaching had on many African nations. He spoke about his work with the non-profit organization to help them with everything from funding to bringing security guards and workers out to help. Then, he asked the people to tell him specifically how he and his organization could help.

Their response: they needed all the help they could get with keeping poachers out, and then dealing with them when they invaded the tribes' land and killed the wildlife.

Patrol guards were needed, and workers too who would build and maintain fencing to keep poachers out. Wildlife experts were needed as well, to work with the wildlife when injured. The tribes needed infrastructure to construct buildings for tourists to come out and see the beauty up close. This would help to build more support for the wildlife, educate more people and start an economy that would sustain rather than destroy the wildlife.

The conversation was going well when a Molotov cocktail came flying through a window, breaking the glass and threatening to set the hall on fire. All instinctively ducked but one security guard, who quickly put the fire out.

A voice came over a bullhorn, "Leave us alone! We're just trying to feed our families!"

Everyone in the building looked at one another in shock. As the smoke cleared, they could hear a vehicle drive off.

In less than a minute, they could hear another vehicle drive up. A different voice came over another bullhorn, "Don't worry, you are safe! Go about your noble work, we will take care of them!"

This was scary. Nobody knew who was in the second vehicle, or who was claiming to protect them.

Joseph explained to Sky that throwing Molotov cocktails and similar acts were not uncommon in Congo; sometimes the violence was much worse. This was just a warning. The Wantu must be prepared for more attacks, more violence, in the future.

Walden worked hard to try to calm both his team and the agitated local people. They had seen this kind of threat before, but never launched directly into a packed community building. That was brazen.

Joseph addressed the crowd, urging them to stand their ground, because this was their way of life and they needed to do all they could for their tribe and the wildlife.

After calm was restored, the community meal was served so everyone was well fed and the locals could share their thoughts with the visitors, who learned more about this Congolese community.

****

At sundown Joseph led the visitors back to their main community three hours away, giving them an opportunity to see the terrain firsthand.

Everyone hung out by the campfires for the last hour or two before going to sleep. Joseph offered to take them on the anti-poaching patrol the following morning. He then introduced Sky and many of the members of his tribe to the visitors, asking that Walden do the same with his contingent.

The professor introduced the teens and where each was from. Then he talked about shared environmental concerns, mentioning something from each person's background that made that person unique.

During the introductions, Sky noticed Kyle, and they started to remember each other. "It's you ... but you're not Sky, you're *Allen*," Kyle said.

"You're Kyle," Sky replied. "Yes, you met me as Allen; but here they named me Sky. That's a long story for later, when we have more time. How's your family recovering from the shooting?"

"Shooting?" Joseph interrupted with concern.

"There was a shooting, at an environmental gathering in Flagstaff, where Kyle's grandfather was killed and his father injured. We were both there." Sky explained.

Joseph and the Wantu were listening intently. Joseph asked, "Is there a connection between that incident and why you fell from the sky?"

Kyle answered before Sky could reply. "There couldn't have been. That was a single gunman who was killed at the site."

Sky started to remember the shooting. He looked at Kyle. The young men instinctively embraced each other. "We will forever have that connection," Sky said.

Kyle nodded. The Wantu smiled at each other, with respect and appreciation that the two were able to openly express their emotions among the group.

Sky noted that while certainly glad to reunite with Kyle, after hearing the introductions he felt they were all brothers and sisters united in a cause.

Joseph handed everybody snacks and *nukunia odela* — that is, pure sweet juice from the fruits of their trees that, in addition to its marvelous flavor, would give the drinkers energy.

Joseph spoke not just about poaching but also about his tribe and their cultural ways.

PoRue was first of the contingent to speak, comparing her culture to that of the Africans. She spoke about the importance of their language and culture.

Kyle chimed in about how culture was a big part of his life.

Lizzy said she didn't know much about Navajo or African culture, but believed in diversity and wanted to learn as much as she could about both.

Cynthia hardly said a word, absorbing everything that everyone else was saying.

Massimo and Janet spoke about the jewelry back home that Massimo's father obtained from visits to different countries here in Africa, saying that they were interested in learning as much as they could about the various local gems and jewelry. Joseph said he would be happy to show them some during their visit.

"Since we're a couple, we're also interested in how couples here go about dating," Massimo admitted with a smile. Janet blushed, saying nothing, but certainly looked interested.

"We're not like some tribes here that have arranged marriages; we just let them meet and let nature take its course," Joseph replied.

Sky added that on the reservations, marriages are not arranged, but it was expected they would marry Native Americans, preferably from their own tribes.

That seemed like a good note on which to end the evening, and everyone went off to sleep. Joseph informed the visitors that except for couples, men and women were separated. So, Massimo and Janet were shown one rondavel, while the other young women and men were shown their respective living quarters.

***

In the morning, as the group was getting ready to leave on patrol, one of the night patrolmen came from over the hill.

"He got them," the man said.

Joseph understood, but before he could reply Sky asked, "Who got whom?"

Joseph explained: Black Robin Hood took out the men who threw the Molotov cocktails into the community center.

"Tell me the particulars," Joseph asked the patrolman.

"About five miles from here, down in the ravine, the poachers were sizing up more wildlife to kill. Black Robin Hood found them. Each had an arrow right through his heart," the patrolman reported, adding that Black Robin Hood left a note for the Wantu: *They won't be bothering you anytime soon with more Molotov cocktails.* The note was signed *BRH*.

Joseph shook his head, not knowing how to respond. Most places in Africa dealing with poachers didn't have anyone to help them with the problem. Now, here was Black Robin Hood helping them. It wasn't the type of help they wanted, but it wasn't help he was going to turn away either.

"The violence doesn't help," Joseph admitted, "but we still have a job to do — so let's load up and do it."

***

For Africans living in Congo and other remote regions, death is a way of life. Due to poachers, colonialists and disease, death at relatively early ages is not at all uncommon. If Africans live to be forty-five, they're considered lucky. They mourn their dead and then get on with their lives.

Rhinos, elephants, zebras and other wildlife all still needed protection, whether or not some individuals had been killed or other wildlife died on any given day.

***

Undeterred by threats and intimidation tactics, the entourage set out: Joseph, the Wantu tribesmen, Dr. Walden and his teenagers, and, of course, the security contingent, all on schedule.

Joseph's driver, Raku, drove for about 45 minutes at a reasonable clip until he had to slow to a crawl so as not to spook the wildlife.

They stopped on a hill overlooking a valley where antelope, zebras and buffalo were grazing peacefully. The visitors watched in awe.

PoRue was taken by the amount of greenery, for there was nothing like it on the Hopi reservation. Cynthia was overwhelmed by all the wildlife they passed in their vehicle. Kyle loved the slowed-down pace here, which amazed him because he was so accustomed to racing and life in the fast lane — though he did reflect on how the slower pace of Africa compared nicely to that of the Navajo.

Massimo and Janet were on jewelry watch, meaning that as the vehicle made its way along, they would look at rocks to see what might be in or near them; but they also kept their eye out for caves they might later explore for minerals.

Lizzy was simply mesmerized by the overall beauty. She would stare into the jungle, wondering what might lurk within and whether that spelled beauty or danger. (In reality, it held both.) And Cynthia, for her part, was taken as well by the overall diversity — of the people and the wildlife, in tandem. That was new to her, so different from anywhere else.

As he did earlier with Sky, Joseph warned the visitors that they needed to train their eyes to notice anything that moves, particularly in or near the bushes.

Moving bushes, he explained, could be wildlife or wind, but it also could be poachers. Being on watch can mean hours or days without anything happening — and it can certainly be tedious — but the moment poachers are seen, it brings chaos. So much can happen in a matter of seconds, he cautioned.

That was how most of the day went. The patrol and the visitors spent hours just watching and enjoying the wildlife and jungle. It was beautiful, mesmerizing and mostly uneventful, with no poachers or other humans in sight.

***

In the late afternoon they began to see a lot of movement in the brush, and there wasn't much wind. Something was up.

Sure enough, from high on a hill, one of the patrol watchers radioed to the group that he could see poachers with submachine guns in a clearing. At least seven of them.

Joseph had several of his patrol fire warning shots into the air to alert the poachers that they'd been seen.

Though heavily armed, the poachers did not want a full-scale shootout in which members of both parties would be killed and wounded. They retreated. When word got back to the Wantu, the tribesmen smiled, knowing the poachers would soon return, whether that night or within two weeks.

The Wantu beefed up their security patrols, their sensors, their lighting and all their fencing, and remained on high alert.

Smitten with the Wantu people and culture, their work to fight poachers and their approach to life, the contingent of teenage environmentalists, along with the professor, decided to extend their time at least a week.

***

The next morning, the security patrol reported back. The seven poachers were all found dead with arrows through their hearts. Black Robin Hood had struck again. Apparently the seven split up at some point, long enough for Black Robin Hood and his arrows to strike.

Again, Joseph shook his head. On the one hand, he was glad to be rid of the poachers, but he wasn't at all happy about the way it was done. There had to be a better way than murder.

The patrols would continue. More poachers surely would come, but for now the Wantu could take a breath, knowing that they and the wildlife were safe for at least a while longer.

Their respite didn't last long. The very next day, poachers were spotted. This time, when warning shots were fired, the poachers did not retreat; nor did they move forward. They just sat, apparently considering their next move.

The poachers then fired their own shots in the air to let the patrol know that they would not retreat. They would be coming — and soon — to get the animals, with elephants and rhinos likely at the top of their list.

Those unambiguous shots in the air meant that both sides now knew the other was there and ready to do battle. The patrol fired more warning shots to let the poachers know that they weren't backing down and would be coming for them.

The poachers were in an open meadow and knew they were sitting ducks if they didn't move fast.

The patrol followed, careful to avoid the poachers' traps. They also wanted to avoid a massacre, and to minimize any casualties that might result from a shootout.

They sent men in all four directions. This worked well, as they had enough soldiers to surround the poachers, who, when they realized all paths were cut off, promptly surrendered. The patrol tied them up and brought them back to camp.

Dr. Walden and his visitors were amazed at what they'd seen in just two days: poachers who'd escaped, only to be hunted down and killed like their prey, and poachers who were captured, bound and brought in.

All were grateful that no large shootout had taken place. So far none of the Wantu had been killed.

That night, as they sat around the campfire eating and drinking, Joseph told the visitors about the different strategies they used to prevent poaching.

Since the bulk of the poaching is to sell the horns — mostly to those who believe they have special powers — one of the strategies was to flood the market with fake horns. The more horns on the market, the less horns people would buy from poachers. This worked to some extent.

Yet, just as some jewelers can always spot a fake, the more astute black marketeers understood right away if horns weren't real.

Another strategy was to trim the rhino horns and elephant tusks. This didn't work at first, but when poachers realized the horns were trimmed it was no longer worthwhile to kill the animal for the little bit that was left.

Joseph told them too about an African public-service campaign to educate people about the benefits of wildlife tourism versus poaching. If successful, the effort would put public pressure on the poachers, which could help to put an end to that billion-dollar industry. The public-service announcements would also make clear that Africans would benefit directly from tourism that emphasized safaris.

"But poachers can still make a lot of money from poaching," Joseph said. "We will continue to prevent and fight poaching however we can."

Joseph pivoted to Massimo, asking the young man to tell him more about the family business. Massimo explained about how his father traveled all over Africa for different types of jewels, and how the jewelry store in New Jersey served as the family's business and Ray's passionate obsession.

"Maybe we can help each other," Joseph said.

"What do you mean?" Massimo asked.

"You and your family know a lot about jewels. We need money for our anti-poaching work."

"I don't understand," said Massimo.

"I feel I can trust you and everyone here," Joseph said quietly. "We must keep this a secret between our tribe and your entourage, because if anyone finds out, the miners and even *more* poachers will come. If that happens, our tribe will be destroyed."

Joseph didn't ask for promises or handshakes because he knew he could trust them. He was happy with their collective nods.

"There is an emerald mine not far from here. Our people know, but no one else. The emerald miners would come out here as quickly as they could if they knew about it. They would decimate our tribe and destroy the land to get the emeralds out. We can get some emeralds out without much problem or work. You could take them back to New Jersey and sell them. You can take some of the proceeds out for your part in this and send us the rest. We would use it in our war. We not only trust you, but we believe that you also support our efforts to stop the poaching and so I believe you will do what's right."

Massimo and the others were stunned by this revelation. A big smile came over Massimo. "When do we start?" he asked.

"We will leave in the morning," Joseph replied.

Sky's eyebrows shot up. He'd been here awhile, he told them, and this was the first he'd heard about the emerald mine.

"You were on a need-to-know basis, and you didn't need to know," Joseph told him, his face solemn.

After a pause, Joseph laughed. He would never be that rude or sarcastic, he assured them. It just wasn't his way. "No, in truth, it just hadn't come up," Joseph told him. "But you will accompany us to the emerald mines. After all, you are now just as one of us."

Now Sky was smiling.

9

Adventure in Emeralds

The Wantu entourage and Dr. Walden's group prepared to leave for the emerald mine in the jeeps, ready to take on the tracks that pass for roads in the jungle.

Joseph broke out a map to show Sky where they were going, as they would be riding together. Several years before, he explained, an anti-poaching team on patrol found what looked to be a handwritten treasure map.

"That is how we found the emerald cave," he told Sky.

On top of the map was scribbled in pen, *"Bright sparkling green cave."*

"We didn't think it was serious — in fact, we thought it was a joke. But we went searching and were amazed to find emeralds in the cave."

The map showed the jungle roads and trails leading to the cave. The part of the map where the cave was located was drawn in bright green pen.

"We drive about ten miles, then walk about three miles, then we have to scramble up about 150 meters to get to the mine," Joseph said.

The patrol was riding along for protection and to look for poachers. Everyone was given a backpack. The packs included water, *nukunia odela*, enough food to last a couple of days (in case they ran into something unforeseen), and tents for overnight, if needed. Each pack also contained a first-aid kit to deal with anything from a snake or spider bite to a gunshot wound. The pack also included knives and guns. The guns in the packs were unloaded, but some in the patrol carried semiautomatics as well.

Joseph wasn't sure whether everyone in Walden's group knew how to handle a weapon. Since the guns were unloaded, he wasn't overly concerned. At least the guns were there if needed, should any of them come under attack.

***

Before they set out, Joseph called everyone together. For his people it was a review of what they were doing. For Sky and the Walden team it was a review of what was in their packs and information about the drive, hike and scramble up to the mine. Joseph asked if anyone was uncomfortable or wanted to stay behind.

"Not a chance. I'm looking forward to the adventure!" Lizzy said.

"Come on, let's go!" said Janet.

The rest all nodded in approval.

Massimo and Janet were most excited about the cave because they were so interested in jewels. The others were excited too, each in their own way.

PoRue was thrilled to simply be there, because till this trip she had never strayed from home. She had only been to Flagstaff and other border towns, and occasionally to Phoenix; until the flight to Africa, she had never left Arizona.

Having been to Phoenix often and toured different parts of the country to race, Kyle was a bit more worldly, but overseas travel was a first for him too, and Congo was an entirely different world, impossible to imagine.

Lizzy had never left Washington. With four kids, any thought of foreign travel seemed remote, at least until the kids were grown. Now, thanks to Ben and the love they shared, this trek was possible. Every minute of the adventure was precious.

Cynthia was mesmerized by the entire experience, and the idea of seeing a cave full of jewels was simply one more wonder.

***

The Wantu, and especially the anti-poaching patrol, were always mindful about what was at stake. They had to take care not only to be on the lookout for poachers, but to be sure they weren't being followed, No one else could know about the mine. This meant covering their tracks.

Along the way Joseph talked about how Africans in general, and their people in particular, have a reverence for Mother Earth. Whether cleaning up after themselves or fighting against those who would defile Her — taking up guns against poachers, for instance, or talking to people who would pollute or litter — for the Wantu this wasn't just a noble cause, it was a calling from a superior being.

PoRue and Kyle nodded, telling Joseph this was similar to their traditions as well. "We pray to the four directions," Kyle told him, while the others keenly listened.

***

The further into the jungle they went, the greener and quieter it became. Apart from the noises of wildlife and the occasional trumpet of an elephant, all was still.

The jeeps crawled along slowly as they kept watch for everything in all four directions.

"Look at that!" The teens would whisper and point as they passed different wildlife along the route. Lizzy mentioned seeing giraffes only in a zoo before coming here. "I like to pet their noses and lightly pinch their lips," she added.

The drive to their stop was uneventful. Joseph showed everyone where the trail would start. They had ten minutes to get ready, just enough time to check their packs and see if they fit, if they were comfortable, and if anyone needed any help.

Joseph checked in with everyone in Walden's group to make sure their packs fit correctly and weren't too heavy to carry.

This short break offered any who needed it a chance to relieve themselves in the bush. Cynthia looked uncomfortable. She hadn't ever done that before, and wasn't sure how she felt about doing it here.

"That's okay," PoRue reassured her. "On the rez some of us don't have bathrooms in our homes. We have to use the outhouse in the back."

"At least it's a *house*," Cynthia said doubtfully.

Once they started the three-mile hike, Joseph explained, it was best not to stop. The plan was to get to the cave as quickly as possible, use whatever time was needed to retrieve a few emeralds, and head back without being seen by anyone.

He also warned them to watch where they walked, where they placed their hands and where they swung their arms. They had to be cautious about snakes and avoid touching trees where insects could bite them, as well as bushes with sharp hidden thorns.

"Sounds scary." Cynthia shuddered.

"You'll be okay as long as you're careful," Massimo assured her.

Janet nodded, "The prospect of emeralds is cool, but we have to get there safely."

***

With Joseph leading the way and the head of the anti-poaching brigade at the rear, the group began their slow hike.

They kept their eyes peeled, not only in each of four directions, but also on the ground and the trees above.

Less than a minute in, the monkeys above started clattering, letting the party know they were invading their homes. They weren't in attack mode, just uncomfortable, as most had never seen humans. The monkeys were more afraid of people than people were of them.

Joseph also advised that they keep their talk to a minimum, and if they must, to whisper.

The weather wasn't hot, but the jungle was humid, so everyone wore either shorts or lightweight pants and tees. Even so, the visitors quickly began to sweat. Joseph reminded them to drink plenty of water to stay hydrated.

They came on an exceptional plant, a tall, green reed with a bright orange flower. The teens all stopped and took photos with their phones, the orange in the flower contrasting so vividly with the background green.

"This is beautiful," Lizzy said, amazed.

"More than beautiful," Joseph said. "We call this flower magic because it quickly heals wounds and cuts."

***

But time was of the essence. Every protocol was being followed to keep the team members safe.

As they moved quietly through the jungle, the brigade listened. Most sounds were from wildlife, but anything that seemed out of place could mean poachers or other intruders.

"It's so quiet here, the opposite of the racetrack," Kyle noted.

They arrived at the base of the small mountain that held the cave. Joseph looked up and the others' eyes followed to the tiny opening near the top. He then looked for the easiest route up.

He whispered that they were ready to start the ascent, and that if anyone had trouble scrambling up the rocks, they could hand their pack to the person ahead. That person then would put the pack down and, making sure they had solid footing, stretch out a hand to help the team member up.

One by one, staying five feet apart in case anyone slipped, they began to make their way up to the cave.

While most of the teens did need a hand, the climb wasn't much of a problem. The dirt path was clear, but the pebbles and smaller rocks were loose, so everyone had to tread lightly. They also had to watch out for plants with prickly ends along the trail, a danger if they reached out without looking.

Once assembled at the cave entrance, the group was reminded to go especially slow and watch for snakes and other creatures, including scorpions, which have painful stings. Joseph also warned of mosquitoes and midges, which are known vectors for many diseases.

Once in the cave, Joseph explained, they would reach the emeralds in ten minutes or so of slow walking.

Each pack had a small flashlight. Joseph instructed them to take out their flashlights and turn them on as soon as the light in the cave grew dim.

Not more than a minute in, Kyle let out a yelp. He'd put his hand on the cave wall to steady himself and a scorpion stung him. Joseph had everyone stop as he retrieved his first-aid kit.

Sky came over to examine the sting. "You are tough one! Guess you have to be, because a lot keeps happening to you," Sky told his friend.

Joseph applied cream to Kyle's hand. "Here, that's better. That will keep you until we get back to camp and put more medicine on it."

"Thanks. I appreciate that, it's soothing," Kyle said, relieved.

***

Although Dr. Walden had been in the bush many times, he knew this was Joseph and Raku's land, so he would typically defer to them, including not just where to go but what to look for and how to take care as well.

The scorpion sting was a wake-up call to what can happen when you don't pay absolute attention. Now the group was on high alert — PoRue especially, who turned white as a ghost the moment Kyle realized he'd been stung. The episode caused her to fall to the back, nearer to Joseph at the tail.

With flashlights now on, they could see multitudes of scorpions and big spiderwebs. They could also see petroglyphs on the walls left by ancient people.

The cave had many blind turns, further winding them in.

"How will we know when we get there?" Sky asked.

Joseph said it would be obvious.

"But how?" Sky persisted.

"Be patient," Joseph urged.

The group kept moving, proceeding slowly through the labyrinthine cave, with flashlights aimed at the walls, ceiling and floor.

They were both intrigued and scared at once.

***

At the fifth corridor, they arrived. By this time Joseph had made his way to the front of the group, where he joined tracker Raku.

The enclosure glowed brilliant green on all sides, with emeralds embedded in the walls. It felt as though they'd entered a room with a hundred bright green lights.

In most movies the precious, sought-after gem is nearly always immense and must be dug out of the ground; but here, the emeralds were among the rocks in the walls, and there were hundreds of much smaller pieces.

A green glow emanated from the cave floor as well, where they spotted a small pool of water. It already glowed green from the emeralds within, but a natural sunroof at the top of the cave, an aperture, let in a shaft of light in that made the pool glow even brighter.

They were in awe. They saw right away that they wouldn't have to dig for the emeralds. They could simply pull them out of the rocky cave walls.

One other thing prominently stood out: straight ahead, in the middle of the wall, was a note attached to one of the larger emeralds that read *Take what you need to fight the poachers, but don't be greedy — and leave no trace.* The note was signed *BRH.*

Clearly, whether intended as one or not, the unknown character had adopted the name Black Robin Hood as a badge of honor.

Joseph read the message aloud, without a thought about how it might affect the group. After all, it contained an implied threat — *don't be greedy* — from a vigilante killer. Even so, it was plain for them to see.

"There really is a Black Robin Hood? I thought that was a fairy tale," said Massimo, eyeing the largest emeralds.

"Black Robin Hood is quite real, I assure you," Joseph said. "He has a sense of humor, but he is deadly serious when it comes to protecting the rhinos, the elephants, and everything he considers his land."

"It sounds like a warning as well," said Janet, noticing where Massimo was looking.

"I'm glad somebody else is here to help," Lizzy said, oblivious to the unspoken danger.

Janet shifted slightly and let out a troubled sigh.

***

Joseph whispered to the group that they each should take ten small pieces of emerald and secure them in their packs. Ten pieces, he explained, weigh about 150 grams in total; while moderate in size, the individual stones didn't weigh much.

Each began to carefully pry the emeralds from the walls, inspecting them and stowing them in their packs. This activity went on without incident until an eerie feeling came over them. They felt the presence of something in the room.

"Scorpions, spiders, what *now?*" Cynthia asked rhetorically.

Then she shined the light behind her and froze: a striped polecat.

Oh no. Joseph's heart sank. Taking care not to startle the creature, he explained in hushed tones that while this animal wasn't deadly, if it did decide to spray, they might wish it were. As with a skunk, polecat spray anywhere close to humans is never good, but here in the cave it would be unbearable.

No one moved. Eight minutes passed. The polecat couldn't seem to make up its mind. It would wander over to where some team members were frozen in place, stop as though alert to a danger — causing panic in their hearts — then move away. The minutes felt like hours. Having apparently decided that humans weren't anything to fear, the polecat eventually went on its way.

"That was close." Kyle wiped sweat off his brow.

Cynthia remained in place, uncertain. "How often does that happen?" she asked. "We really don't need *that* to happen again."

"If one puny onion burns my eyes and turns them into non-stop waterworks, what would getting skunked up close be like in a cave?" Janet sounded upset.

Joseph said they shouldn't linger. The polecat could reappear at any time — as could other wild animals. The adventurers wasted no time. They carefully secured the emeralds as instructed, being sure not to rush and to observe the protocols.

They finished in about fifteen minutes and started their descent back to the jungle trail.

***

Once they were down from the emerald cave, the group assembled to make sure everyone was there. A quick head count showed that PoRue was missing.

Massimo said he wondered why he didn't hear or see her when everybody else was whispering in the cave. Maybe she ran when the polecat showed up? Maybe she needed to visit the bush?

Joseph told everyone to be quiet. He listened for any sound, any clue; all he could hear was the wind.

"We need to stick together," Joseph said. "If someone took her and we go after her one by one, we would be easy pickings for them."

The patrol took out their guns.

"You don't need to do that yet, but be ready," Joseph advised the rest of the team.

Walden looked stricken, overcome with concern. "We-we need to find her," was all he could manage to say.

The trails were thick with trees to each side, so there wasn't much of view of the terrain. Nor could they tell whether they were being watched.

"How on earth are we going to find her?" Kyle asked. He was only used to wide open space on his Native Navajo desert, not the jungle, so thick with trees that you couldn't see five feet.

Apart from the trail they had taken to the cave, there weren't many others; yet there were game trails, not wide, but enough for people to use in several different directions.

Joseph and Raku were experienced trackers, with years of experience following the movements of poachers.

"Here's the start of their marks," Raku said. "The marks are from PoRue and three adults."

Everyone in the group let out a sigh. The good news was that PoRue was alive. The bad news: she had been kidnapped.

What could the kidnappers want? With no phone service in the jungle, how could they even make contact?

"Let's follow the tracks," Joseph said.

Raku led the way, Walden right behind. The patrolmen were spread through the group, their guns drawn. Joseph took up the rear. That way the group leaders could make sure that no one else was taken.

***

Joseph called a huddle. He especially wanted to talk with Walden and his team.

"Hope. Hope. Hope. You cannot give up hope. That is what we have learned about these kidnappings. We almost always get our children back when they are kidnapped, and that has happened many times. But we cannot get them back if we are not thinking right. We cannot get them back if we panic. Our enemies, the kidnappers, count on us panicking, not thinking right and not taking the right strategies. You must tell yourselves that you are the light in the darkness and you will overcome."

With Raku as their leader, he told them, first they would track the kidnappers. Once they got close, they would lie in wait. One of the kidnappers, sooner or later, would have to go into the bush to pee.

"No place else in the jungle to do that."

"Ugh." Cynthia shuddered.

Once one of them separated from his group, the Wantu would grab him and begin the interrogation to figure out how to capture the other kidnappers without bringing harm to PoRue.

That was the plan. It would rain soon, meaning that they had to get a bead on the kidnappers now, before the deluge washed away their tracks. Raku went about this methodically but quickly. He knew he didn't have much time.

***

As they moved through the jungle, the visitors couldn't help but be overwhelmed with fear and beauty. So long as they kept moving, they believed they were somewhat safe. Even so, the teens were startled by a giant cape buffalo, and gasped when a fish eagle swooped in to snatch its prey.

"That bird is huge!" Kyle gawped at the enormous wingspan.

Most were preoccupied with thoughts of PoRue to worry too much about their safety. The jungle humidity only added to the tension.

Joseph's concern was not just for PoRue but for his visitors as well. Proper thinking and strategy were paramount. It wouldn't do for any to come unglued. These were innocents, he knew, in the ways of kidnappers. He needed to keep them focused.

Joseph pointed to a dainty and lovely sable antelope.

"In the bush, there is beauty as well as ugly. In the bush, there is good side-by-side with evil," he consoled them.

***

Raku confirmed that three men had taken PoRue, and figured that they assumed the rest of her people didn't know she was taken and they had a good head start — so far ahead, they thought, that even if her group started tracking them, they would never catch up this late in the day.

"We must keep moving," Joseph told the group.

Raku's experience and skill at tracking was second to none. Once he found the initial track, he would be able to follow even if the traces were covered up. The three kidnappers didn't even bother.

***

The African sun started going down.

The kidnappers decided to stop for the night and make camp. This was a mistake. If they had forged ahead into total darkness, the Wantu trackers may not have been able to find them.

Raku was not only a good physical tracker but had a sense of where to follow when all tracks stopped — because he knew where *he* would continue, even if he'd never set foot there.

That sense kicked in with certainty when the people he was following stopped.

Raku held up his hand and everyone in the group halted.

"They are not far ahead of us. Everyone put your packs down and rest. Our enemies are near," he told them. "Joseph and four of my men will come with me. The rest of you stay here, but keep alert and watch each other. We don't need anybody else taken by kidnappers or animals."

Massimo protested, saying he wanted to go with the crew to rescue PoRue, but Joseph convinced him that he needed to stay behind to help protect the others.

Walden agreed and knew that he too had to stay with the people he'd brought in to make sure they stayed calm and safe.

Janet was happy to know that Massimo would remain behind.

Lizzy worked hard at keeping calm. Overwhelmed by what was happening, she was doing her best not to panic because she didn't want to make the situation any worse for the others.

Kyle quietly accepted the orders. He also wanted to help his group as much as he could.

Sky, though, insisted on accompanying the away team. Joseph at first resisted but ultimately agreed because he felt Sky's martial arts training could help, especially if it came down to hand-to-hand combat.

"You could make the difference," Joseph told him. "We need any edge we can get."

***

Joseph believed that the kidnappers were more focused on getting away than covering their tracks.

Within a half hour, Raku and his party came to a cliff overlooking the meadow where the three men set up camp for the night with their prisoner.

"Spread out and wait," Raku instructed his men. They knew his plan was under way.

As a precaution, the kidnappers did not light a fire, but they had no idea they were followed.

Using his heightened sense, Raku had a good idea where one of them would go to relieve himself. He lay in wait like a tiger patiently stalking a deer, allowing it to roam, to go to its natural place.

Sure enough, after forty-five minutes one of the kidnappers took off down a game trail to urinate — where Raku was waiting. Creeping up behind the man, Raku put a large knife to his throat and whispered that one wrong move or sound would be the end of him.

The man, looking terrified, nodded his head. Then he found enough courage to whisper back that if they tried to rescue the girl, his friends would kill her on the spot.

By now, Joseph and two others had joined them. They bound the man's arms and legs.

"We will castrate you and cut you inch by inch if you don't give us the information we want," Raku promised.

The man's eyes bulged with fear.

He gave close, do you want to know?"

"How many others in the group?"

"Two."

"What type of weapons do they have?"

"Automatic guns, handguns, knives."

"Why did they take her?"

"They will sell her, maybe as a slave for prostitution."

"Who is paying you?"

"Only my boss knows that, but they would have to take her to the city," he explained.

"How can you do this? Don't you realize the terror that you're inflicting on people? Don't you realize how wrong this is?"

"I feel bad about it, I do! but this is the only way I can feed my family. There are no jobs anywhere near here and no way for my family to leave."

"Don't you realize the danger you put yourself in? There is a good chance you will die or go to prison. Then what will your family do?"

The kidnapper broke down in tears.

"I felt like I had no choice."

Joseph shook his head in disbelief that this kidnapper saw no other way.

***

At this point, Joseph and Raku tied the kidnapper's mouth as well as his hands, arms and legs.

They knew they had to act quickly because if they didn't, the kidnappers would catch on and either kill PoRue on the spot or try taking off into the bush. The original plan was to wait for total darkness and then pounce, but now to wait was too risky.

They outnumbered the kidnappers six to two, but if they were too straightforward in their approach, the kidnappers could gun them down with semiautomatic weapons.

Joseph and Raku were excellent marksmen with their knives. The others in the group weren't bad with knives either, so they decided to use those in a stealth attack rather than noisy guns. The kidnappers were sitting outside, eating and talking with PoRue in between them. PoRue's hands and feet were tied. One told the other he would feed her by hand after they were done eating.

"We have to keep her pretty," he said.

The plan was that Joseph and Raku both would throw knives at the kidnappers' heads with the intent of killing them before any harm could be done to PoRue. If they missed, others in their crew would be ready with knives of their own and guns if needed.

Raku's knife was true, hitting the man square in the head and killing him instantly; but Joseph's knife was totally off, missing to the right. The remaining kidnapper's instincts kicked in and he grabbed PoRue along with his machete and placed it to her throat.

Joseph, Raku and the rest of the team now knew that any wrong movement would mean PoRue's death.

They had no sure way of saving her. Each had his own thoughts about what to do next, but they all knew that any move came with a risk.

"Can we talk about it?" Joseph called out to the kidnapper.

"Why do you want to do that? How can we resolve this?" The kidnapper responded. "I know you want this girl alive or you would not have come after her, but if you kill me, then she will surely die. So, what do you propose?"

Before Joseph could answer, they heard a whooshing sound. An arrow, through the air and into one side of the kidnapper's head, coming out the other. He was killed instantly, without so much as a scratch on PoRue.

Black Robin Hood had struck, and like the wind, he was gone.

***

PoRue fell to the ground in grief and tears. Raku, Joseph and the others rushed over. They untied her as quickly as possible. Joseph hugged PoRue as if she were his own, as if he'd known her their entire lives. He treated her just as he would his own daughter.

Sky also rushed over and hugged PoRue. "I cannot let anything happen to my sister," he said, holding her tight.

Then to the matter of the prisoner. They untied his legs so he could walk, but they kept his hands and arms bound tightly. He had no way of escape: even if he managed to free himself, he had no water, no food, no flashlight and no weapon with which to survive in the jungle.

Even with flashlights, it took them more than an hour to get back. As they came upon the others, as soon as she saw them, PoRue broke out running, straight into Kyle's arms.

Overcome with happiness and surprise, Kyle hugged her back, as he would a long-lost lover.

"I think we're safe tonight," Joseph interrupted the joyful homecoming. "But let's start back — and if we talk along the way, *please* let's keep it to a whisper — I don't want to throw any more knives."

10

Endangered Species

In the morning everyone came together for breakfast to chill out and discuss the kidnapping.

"Let me show you something. Follow me. You can bring your *nukunia odela* or your coffee," Joseph beckoned Walden and his teens.

They followed him to an enclosure in back of the area with the rondavels, blocked off by trees so no one could see in. The enclosure, containing many kinds of wildlife, was heavily surrounded by Wantu armed guards.

"These are our endangered species, and we would protect them with our lives. We *do* protect them with our lives," Joseph said. "We protect them in two ways. First, we pray for them. Second, we defend them physically. The poachers will come for them if they find out they're here — so we guard them. Even so, at some point — and we can never know when — the poachers may try to take us."

"Wow. What have we here?" Sky peered into the enclosures, elaborately fenced to keep species apart. These tall structures prevented attacks by predators, and to keep injured animals from going where predators could get at them.

Joseph explained, and Walden joined him. The professor had done his homework: in Congo, he told them, there are five endangered species, nine vulnerable species and four threatened species. Endangered species are at the highest risk, vulnerable species at high risk, and threatened species likely to become high risk in the near future.

"These are our endangered species — all injured or wounded." Joseph pointed to the animals in the enclosure. All would have died, he explained, had they been left in the wild. While perhaps not fitting the precise definition, if any are in danger of dying, the Wantu consider them endangered.

Here were white rhinos, elephants, leopards, zebras, hyenas, bush babies and many other types. Here too were variously colored birds, and bats of all sizes. The enclosure contained as well an exotic variety of duikers and antelope.

"Not all of these are on anyone's endangered list. Some, are, and some are more endangered than others, but we don't differentiate because if any of them become endangered or extinct, it impacts the entire food chain and may cause the extinction of many others, including humans," Joseph elaborated. "But the white rhino is special. You know it can hardly see, so it depends on smell for all that it does."

The teens all were listening, rapt.

"As Wantu, here in the jungle we have many beliefs," he continued. "One belief is that there is good and bad; not much in between because when you stray from good that will get you killed. We also believe that all life is related: not just all people and all animals, but also the plants, the rocks, the mountains. When one suffers, all suffer."

Kyle interrupted to say that his Navajo people have similar beliefs. Sky nodded in agreement.

"We also believe in magic," Joseph said.

"What kind of magic?" PoRue asked, following the conversation closely.

"The magic of good and bad spirits," Joseph replied. "These good and bad spirits are held in humans and in the wildlife. In most cases, it is obvious, such as the poachers, who are bad, and the anti-poachers, who are fighting against their evil; but sometimes these spirits aren't as obvious, as the people or wildlife are not what they seem. Sometimes they can also be changed, like a poacher who is captured and learns about our ways and comes over to our side. Or an anti-poacher who, for some sort of quick gratification, goes over to the evil side."

Massimo's dad often talked about the jewelry and other parts of African life, but always steered clear of getting involved in African culture or politics. That was *their* business, he'd say. This whole philosophy Massimo was now learning about was new. "So how do *you* deal with the forces of evil?" Massimo asked.

"We have medicine men to guide us. Some call them shamans. Some call them wizards, but these are spiritual leaders who guide us and counter the forms of bad magic," Joseph answered. "They are our guardian angels. They protect Mother Earth and all living beings."

Sky said he saw similarities between the medicine men on Hopi and the medicine men here. Sky also spoke about how the Hopi people liked to plan seven generations ahead, to preserve everything for those future generations.

***

These enclosures, Joseph said, were set up by the Wantu for the injured wildlife about ten years before. A veterinarian, employed to train the staff on how to work with these animals, returned once a month or whenever special treatment is needed.

The tribe's future depended on the survival of these species: without them, safaris and all the revenue they brought in would dry up. By preserving and caring for the endangered species, the Wantu not only protect them but offer people an appreciation for the wildlife and a place where the tribe can earn enough to become more sustainable.

"This will help us improve our quality of life," Joseph said. "We can make more from having a safari resort with outings than than the poachers can make from their bad deeds. Then we can use the money to help the wildlife.

"You look at what the writer Lawrence Anthony did with his resort and the thousands of animals he helped. Amazing! If we can copy that well, we'll be just fine and the world will be a better place. Yesterday we saw the jewels that you call emeralds; later today you will see *our* jewels: the wildlife. So, start getting your packs ready, we will leave after lunch."

***

The group here was learning more in one week than they would from a year in college.

Back at the main camp, they met to go over the plans before heading out.

"I hope this isn't anything like yesterday." PoRoe shuddered.

Joseph told her not to worry: the jungle guardian angels would be looking out for them — adding that while they shouldn't be afraid, they should always be attentive to everything around them. That meant looking out for poachers and wildlife that saw them as prey, and being mindful of snakes and other poisonous creatures.

"You have to be attentive to the weather. We are just entering the rainy season. The sky can be totally blue and fifteen minutes later the clouds can move in and it can rain really hard. That's why you need to make sure your raincoats are in your packs. Make sure your first-aid kits are in there as well. Always doublecheck that your knives and matches are in your pack. In the jungle, not being prepared can mean injury or death."

PoRue and Kyle tried to keep their hormones in check as they did not want to draw any undue attention, but it was clear they wanted to be with each other. They had inched closer together while Joseph was speaking.

"What do you think?" PoRue asked Kyle.

"This is wonderful. This is a once-in-a-lifetime chance to see something that most people won't ever see," he responded.

"Do you want to keep talking, or do you want to get ready to go?" Joseph asked, giving them the nudge to go check their packs. The plan was for everyone to load up, eat lunch, and then the entourage would set out to see the endangered species.

The Wantu team, Walden's group and the anti-poachers loaded up the mud-covered jeeps and started toward the jungle, with Joseph, Sky and Walden in the lead vehicle. The soldiers were in the front and back of every jeep with the teens. Raku was in the last vehicle, keeping a lookout for poachers and other danger.

About five miles down the road, they came across a herd of okapi.

"That's different," Massimo said. "Its head looks like a dog, its body looks like a horse, and its backside looks like a zebra."

"It's unique," Joseph said. "It's related to the giraffe."

The jeeps stopped to give everyone a chance to enjoy seeing the okapi as the visitors took photos and videos with their phones. Not far from the herd they could see a number of small rodents moving in the bush. Massimo borrowed Joseph's binoculars.

"They're so tiny," he observed.

Joseph told Massimo that he was watching dwarf scaly-tailed squirrels — about one-third a normal squirrel's size. A few more minutes here and they were off.

Ten minutes down the road, they came to a large open meadow with a herd of elephants, zebras and blue duikers grazing. The land here was flat, and on the other side of the meadow they could see a tributary of the Congo River. Hippopotamuses were bathing while crocodiles moved around them as if the hippos weren't there. Everyone took in the scene with awe.

The visitors had seen elephants, zebras, hippos and crocodiles on TV and in zoos, but none had ever seen a blue antelope before. The blue duiker is blue and gray, but the blue stood out.

"Is that real?" Kyle asked.

"Very real. We don't know what makes them blue, but they are so blue. It is a phenomenon indeed," Joseph said.

Joseph explained that the blue duiker is endangered due to loss of habitat from loggers and miners who destroyed much of the land. The visitors noticed that this small antelope was not much bigger than a medium-sized dog. Blue duikers are known for eating fruit, flowers and bark — in other words, not meat eaters. They also have flat heads, but with sharp horns to protect against predators.

Joseph looked at the sky and saw clouds moving in. Not many, but they were gray to black. When they moved, they often did so quickly and would blot out the sun, plunging them in darkness. Then, just as quickly, they would move off and all would be bright Congo light.

Joseph paused, then announced they had to move on. He wanted them to see the white rhinos and other species, so they had to go deeper into the jungle. The clouds didn't look scary at that moment, but he knew that could change.

They started down the narrow jeep track when a wildebeest stopped and decided to sit, right in the middle of the road, leaving no room to go around. It reminded some of them of the scene in *Crocodile Dundee*, where the bull, similarly situated, simply won't budge.

"We cannot work miracles like Crocodile Dundee," Joseph said to the group.

Yet he had something more practical in mind. He produced a bullhorn just for this purpose, jumped out of the jeep and came within five feet of the wildebeest, making sure to keep in front of the vehicle. Then he blasted the bullhorn. The wildebeest jumped up, stared at him for a second or two, then slowly started off into the forest, ruffling the spiky sharp tree branches as though they barely existed.

Now they were moving just a tad faster and kept on for another thirty minutes when they spotted a lion on the side of the road rubbing itself up against a tree.

"That's really unusual, to see a lion during the day," Joseph said.

"Look at that! It's beautiful," Sky marveled.

"I'm not sure whether to be in awe or scared," said Lizzy.

Janet, the quietest one on this trip, was breathing hard with excitement.

"The lion is scary and majestic at the same time," she whispered.

***

"Janet has the right idea: keep your voices down," Joseph cautioned. "This is marvelous, but we don't want him charging the jeep." He paused, relishing the moment. "We shouldn't linger too long, but this, my friends, is special indeed."

PoRue and Kyle quietly recounted how they had seen lions in zoos, but this was so totally different. *This* was the once-in-a-life-time experience they sought. The lion looked at them and let out a roar, but then turned away with a look of indifference. Then it ran off into the forest so swiftly and with so much grace that it was like a dream, almost as if it never happened.

"That was the coolest thing I ever saw," Cynthia said.

Janet nodded in agreement. "Will we ever see anything like that again?" she asked.

Sky shook his head in wonder. "We have mountain lions on Hopi, but nothing like that!"

Those who weren't struck dumb or who didn't simply stare had the wherewithal to capture it on video, while others took quick photos, knowing their friends back home would never believe they were this close to a lion if they didn't have proof.

Onward. More clouds were coming, thicker and darker.

"We must keep moving. There are three more species I want you to see before we head home. We have come this far and we only have three more stops. During the first stop, we will see bonobos; and for the second stop, gorillas. Then for our last stop we will see rhinos. You have seen white rhinos already on this trip, but this is a special group, with one really special rhino.

"You don't have many days left before you head home and we are entering the rainy season, so each day may become tougher to get into the jungle. Once the heavy rains come and the mud hits, these jeep roads are often impassable," Joseph said. "Anyone want to turn back?"

The teenagers gave Joseph a look like the question was crazy. Nobody said anything, but he knew their answer. Sky remained quiet, knowing that he planned to stay longer than the visiting group. Joseph knew that as well, and so treated Sky as a fellow Wantu.

Walden had safety in mind at all times, but he also knew that many in this group would never see Congo again. This was one of the main reasons they were here. They had to see what they had to save: the rhinos and the wildlife. Walden believed that the more the teens saw of the wildlife and the land, the more they would be motivated to work toward saving everything in Congo.

Joseph informed them that they would ride for another twenty minutes or so, then they would put on their packs. A ten-minute walk would take them down to the river, where they would see the bonobos; then they would be off to see the gorillas.

Every one of the visitors looked like little kids at Christmas. They couldn't wait to unwrap their packages.

"What are bonobos?" Lizzy asked. "It sounds like chocolate."

Kyle just grinned at her. Joseph chuckled.

Walden said he would answer that one. He told them that bonobos were like chimpanzees but smaller, less than four feet tall. They were slimmer than chimpanzees, with flailing arms — kind of like the Gumby of the jungle. He said the oddest quirk about the bonobos is that while many other apes become violent if they have conflicts with other apes, bonobos revert to sex.

PoRue couldn't help but giggle. "Maybe humans should copy them," she suggested.

The others gave PoRue an odd look.

"Don't you think sex is better than violence?" she asked the group.

Walden said that in the animal kingdom this was true. Sky just scratched his head. Joseph said both were part of life.

The not so funny part about bonobos, the professor added, is that they are endangered mostly due to habitat loss and poaching, although crocodiles do eat them.

Joseph's timing was right on the money: exactly twenty minutes to the trail. By now, the clouds were getting even darker and it was drizzling. Just lightly.

"Hopefully, we can get this done without problems," said Joseph. "Everybody has five minutes to get their packs and do what you have to do. Once we start, no stopping till we get down to the river, but it will only be about ten minutes."

PoRue asked Kyle for help with her pack.

"Anything for attention." Massimo snickered.

Janet smiled but put her own pack on without help — and made a show of it, for the others. "Kids!" Sky laughed, shaking his head at his fellow teens.

Walden encouraged them to get their act together.

"You have a good group. You don't have to worry," Cynthia said.

He said he still felt the need to repeat it.

Sure enough, all were ready in five minutes, even those who needed bathroom breaks. The teens knew there was danger in the jungle, but they were okay with the risks, it was part of the deal.

Again, the trail wasn't much wider than a game trail, and trees covered the sides. The leaves were thick and the trees were tall enough, but these trees had flat tops. Not something you would see in an American forest.

Joseph was right about the time. If the weather was good, sometimes he'd linger to observe the wildlife, the plants and the trees; but if the weather was questionable — as it was today — the goal was to always keep moving.

"Wow." Kyle, a step behind Joseph, stopped in his tracks and stared.

They'd come to an opening in the forest, and a meadow about a hundred feet away, with the Congo River gushing and about thirty bonobos drinking from the water, playing in the flat-topped trees above and eating berries from nearby bushes. Most of them were playing. Some were having sex (maybe, thought PoRue, they were mad at each other?).

Joseph walked far enough down to the path so that everyone could emerge from the forest trail and see the bonobos along with the thundering river — thundering because it was moving so fast. The sky was now almost totally dark, but no thunder or lightning, yet.

Now everyone stopped to take in the moment. Next, of course, out came the phones to document the moment. Joseph told them to keep their movements slow so as not to scare the bonobos. After a few moments, soaking it all in, they proceeded slowly toward the water.

"See the plank." Joseph pointed.

A plank of wood was positioned across the fast-moving river so that people could cross.

"Everybody gather around me so I don't have to speak loudly," Joseph said.

They listened.

"This is what we'll do. We have to cross over the plank to get to the trail on the other side. The plank is large enough for every-body, but we can't take any chance of anybody falling because the river can wash you away in a heartbeat, so we'll lock arms and walk slowly across the plank."

They understood.

Joseph went first, locking arms with Walden, then Kyle was next in line. PoRue slipped in next to him. One by one, the others locked arms.

After PoRue, the soldiers locked arms in between each of the teens to ensure that no one fell in. Raku would be last, to see that everyone made it across okay.

As they started across the plank, the bonobos sounded off. The apes were in the flat-topped trees on both sides of the rushing river, and some in the branches bending over it. The bonobos kept it up, their shrieks getting louder and louder, as they felt the humans were invading their territory. Between the bonobos' screams and the thundering of the river the sounds were almost deafening.

The footbridge was slick from constant splashing. Even though the party all linked arms, Lizzy's hands, legs and feet became so wet that she slipped right through the soldiers' grip and tumbled into the river.

Had she not caught herself on a protruding boulder, Lizzy would have been swept away in the rapid current; yet with both arms clinging fast to the rock and head held barely above water, she could only just hang on — but not for long.

Everyone seemed stunned, frozen in the moment, not knowing precisely what to do.

Lizzy's mind flashed to her kids and Ben.

"Do something!" Sky yelled out, to anyone who could possibly save her.

"I can do this," Janet told them.

Using her climbing skills, Janet walked sideways along the logs, limber toes gripping them firmly, then stuck out her arm and told Lizzy to grab it.

Lizzy, almost too afraid, sucked in her breath, closed her eyes, and grabbed for dear life. Janet hoisted her up, caught her deftly around the waist and pulled Lizzy safely onto the logs.

"No time to stop now," Joseph warned.

The rest took only minutes to cross, and once they reached the other side, all plunked themselves down on the ground.

Then, when it hit her, Lizzy broke down and started crying. Between sobs, all she could manage was to say "th-thank you" over and over to Janet.

PoRue came over and gave them both bear hugs. "You put a scare into us!" She laughed.

Massimo grimaced. *"Whew!"* was all he could say.

Joseph approached. "Take this," he said to Lizzy, handing her a ball of turquoise that looked as though it once had been a flower.

"What is that?" she asked.

"Something to calm your nerves."

Lizzy swallowed it in one great gulp.

"I needed that," she said to the group.

A much-needed wave of relief flooded over them.

"That was supposed to be the easy part," Joseph said.

"Like on Hopi," Sky added, "nothing comes easy, but it's worthwhile."

***

They would have about two minutes, Joseph announced, to catch their breath and then begin the next part of their journey: the thirty-minute walk to see the gorillas.

"When we get there," Joseph warned, "you have to be very quiet. You don't want to spook the gorillas. The gorillas are peaceful, but if you scare them, if you make them think you might hurt their young, they can kill you with one swipe. Sometimes when they see humans, they want to play with them. They may swipe at people playfully, but not knowing their own strength, can accidentally kill us. Take it seriously."

"Do gorillas have sex when they get mad?" Massimo asked, to lighten the moment.

"I don't think so, but you can watch to figure that out for yourself when we get there," Joseph said archly.

With that, they started slowly down the trail. Though the teens had been here only a few days, they'd become accustomed to the exotic jungle trails. The Navajo reservation, New Jersey and Seattle, so different from one another in hiking and trails, at least

191

shared this or that topographical feature, yet nothing that resembled the African jungle. Navajo has little water; New Jersey and Seattle have beautiful lakes and streams; nowhere, though, in the United States was there anything like the Congo River.

The light rain continued. Joseph didn't want to let the teens down, and though he knew the rainy season was here, this was their last chance to see the gorillas and then, hopefully, the white rhinos.

Out came the ponchos, in case the rain started coming down harder. Some in the group put them on.

Everyone in the party — teens and soldiers — kept their eyes wide for any kind of danger, but they could take care and keep a good pace without wasting a precious moment. Their goal was to see as much as they could before the weather forced them to turn back.

The half-hour trek proceeded without problems. Joseph hushed them all and silently pointed to the right, near a cluster of trees.

"That's amazing!" Lizzy whispered, seeing a family of about twenty gorillas.

"They're *huge!*" Cynthia said.

"Look at how slow they move," Kyle whispered.

"But gentle most of the time," Joseph noted.

Indeed, the gorillas were playing gently. They weren't as active as the smaller bonobos. The adult gorillas were about four hundred pounds each. If they stood straight up (which none did), they would be about seven feet tall. The big gorillas were cuddling their little ones.

"It's a wonder they don't crush the young ones," Lizzy said. "They're really hairy. Would you look at those teeth?"

She was referring to the gorillas' big smiles when they played with one another. They would show their teeth that would appear super white, as though they'd just come from the dentist.

"Don't be taken in by those teeth," Joseph said, his voice low. "If they bite you, that would seriously injure you or even kill you, but it is highly unusual for a gorilla to bite a human. If they come after you, they will be swatting you with their arms."

"Their size is intimidating but their demeanor is not," Janet observed in wonder.

The group watched the gorillas as they foraged and sat to eat. They were munching on bananas, berries, green leaves and seeds.

"The gorillas are integral to the jungle's ecosystem," Joseph explained. "They eat the seeds and at some point, poop them out, which spreads the seeds all over the place, giving plants more chance to grow everywhere. While the gorillas eat mostly fruits and seeds, they also eat ants and rodents, keeping them from becoming too prolific."

Some of the gorillas would get tired of playing and roll over to take a nap. No matter how often he saw them, Joseph remained in awe of the gorillas, but he was having even more fun watching the visitors so entranced. The plan was to stay a while longer, but then the rain started in earnest.

All at once it began to pour. Those wearing ponchos buttoned them. Others, now soaked, grabbed them from their packs. The light sprinkle of the past few hours burst into heavy rain.

"It usually doesn't rain this hard for very long," Joseph said.

But it did. The rain came down harder and harder. Lightning and thunder added to the drama. The lightning came bright, fast and close. The thunder was so loud, none could hear anyone over the din.

Then, a huge bang and lightning lit up the sky. The group was frightened. They were right next to a family of gorillas. How would the gorillas react should the lightning strike?

Joseph motioned everyone to huddle.

"Gorillas don't usually respond to thunder and lightning," he quickly explained. "They usually just continue to forage and play during storms, although they might go into a nearby cave or enclosure. One thing they know is not to stay near trees in case they get hit by lightning."

True to form, the gorillas continued to forage, but the thunder became so loud and the lightning so extreme that they paused, at which point one of them locked eyes with the group.

Then he charged.

It was terrifying — then just as suddenly he stopped, about five feet away, and simply stared at them. He turned away, clearly bored, and returned to his group. The gorillas all went back to foraging and playing, despite the pounding rain.

Too stunned to move, the visitors let out a collective breath. No way could they have outrun him.

"That made all the hair on my back stand up," Kyle said.

"I think it made the hair on my back fall *off*," Massimo responded.

"It's been lovely," Janet said, "but let's please get out of here."

"Amen," PoRue chimed in. Then another great flash of lightning struck, about twenty feet away.

"There's a cave," Joseph told them, "ten minutes from here. We will go there till the rain lets up."

"Oh no — not another cave!" PoRue fearfully objected.

"Settle down. We'll keep a special eye on you," Kyle promised.

"You always keep a special eye on her. This time I'll watch her too," Janet said.

They had to proceed with utmost care, Joseph said, so they would not get lost in the rain. Kyle was to walk in front of PoRue and Janet in back, so that PoRue would feel safe. He also assigned one member of the brigade to keep an eye on the professor and each of the teens. Everyone had to stay close.

The ten-minute walk turned into a twenty-minute walk thanks to mud. At last, they arrived and entered the cave. Everyone was soaked, but once inside they all sighed with relief.

"What's happening to me? I-I'm sinking!" Walden said, with a note of panic.

"It's quicksand," Joseph said calmly but urgently.

"It's okay, we have time" Sky quickly pulled a rope from his pack. He lassoed the professor and tried to haul him in, but the resistance and draw of the quicksand was too much, so he motioned the others over to help. All ran to the rope and started pulling as though it was a tug of war. Even with everyone throwing their backs into it, the job went slowly, but eventually they were able to pull him out.

Walden was a mess.

"Thank you all! I'm eternally grateful!" he said, wiping as much of the mud off as he could.

"When I get home, I swear I'm never going into a cave again!" PoRue vowed.

"I'm starting to feel strange about them too," said Janet.

"We're all safe, and we're going to stay that way," Sky affirmed.

Everyone moved far enough into the cave to avoid getting wet, but stayed near enough to the mouth to watch the rain. It was really pouring. The thunder and lightning continued to sound and strike as though the jungle gods were putting on a special show just for them.

The birds had been very loud when the downpour started, but quickly quieted; now the elephants and hyenas were sounding off. When the group entered the cave, it was clear that it was home to bats, and on sensing the humans the bats flew deeper in.

"Let's wait awhile and see if it lets up," Joseph said, looking out.

Walden and the teens chatted about their incredible day so far; but, they wondered, would they get to see the tribe's beloved white rhinos?

Joseph, Raku and the soldiers stayed quiet. For one, they were entertained by listening to what the visitors thought of the Wantu home and their wildlife. They were also watching intently for anything dangerous, whether human, animal or nature itself.

The thunder continued to boom nonstop and the lightning was so strong that it lit up the cave. They stood and looked out, waiting for relief.

About an hour passed. Joseph had seen enough. The storm showed no sign of letting up.

"We will stay here tonight. Even during the thick of the rainy season, it doesn't rain in the morning, so we will get up at sunlight, eat breakfast and go see the rhinos," Joseph said. "We will head back in the early afternoon tomorrow, before the rain starts up again. So, get your bedrolls out."

Sky was first to break out in a smile. "I didn't see that coming, but it makes me happy. Rain brings good luck and good spirits!"

"Our adventure continues," said Janet, with an ominous feeling.

The rest of the teens were beaming: their mission to see the white rhino was on!

Joseph said that he was glad they were happy, but they needed to know a few things before they turned in for the night. The two issues he wanted to talk to them about: global warming and red ants.

"Some people don't believe in global warming," he began. "But if you live in the African jungle, you know it's real. It gets hotter and hotter every year. There is less rain every year, and when rains come, they are more torrential."

Sky noted this was also true on the Navajo and Hopi Reservations. PoRue and Kyle were nodding in agreement. Lizzy recalled that even in Seattle, known for its lush greenery, it just wasn't as wet as it used to be. Massimo and Janet said that while

New Jersey was also hotter, they seemed to be having more floods.

"It's happening — the flooding — all the time now."

All took a moment to reflect. Walden described the situation in his state, Arizona: how, despite more than twenty years of drought, the state and most of Arizona's cities continued to allow the spread of housing developments.

He lamented that neither the state legislature nor governor would do anything meaningful to slow the growth or even address the dire water situation.

"All we can do is control what *we* do," the professor said. "We have to use less fossil fuel and less nuclear energy. We have to use less water, and recycle what we can."

Janet said that when she got home, she would be sure to attend youth forums on global warming. She much admired climate-change activist Greta Thunberg, and wanted to see how she could help.

Sky chimed in that humans had to be kind to Mother Earth in any way they could.

Walden said helping Mother Earth and dealing with global warming meant they also had to elect officials to city, state and national offices who care about the environment — and not how energy companies and developers will profit.

PoRue mentioned the many environmental groups on the Navajo Nation and how she planned to work with them, especially with regard to cleaning up the uranium mines. She especially had in mind a group called Don't Nuke the Climate.

Kyle offered to help here as well — no surprise where PoRue was involved.

Massimo and Janet, on their return, planned to join the Sierra Club.

Lizzy said she would work at protecting Seattle's wilderness areas.

***

"Now, about the red ants," Joseph said.

Everybody was attentive, wondering why red ants were suddenly a concern.

Joseph paused. "The red ants come out at night in caves," he told them.

"Eew!" Lizzy erupted, turning white.

Janet squirmed, instantly checking her arms.

"But we have found a solution. You won't necessarily like it. The bite of the red ant can hurt and leave a big red spot. Trust me, you don't want that. I have some garlic powder. After you all are tucked in, Raku will sprinkle plenty of the garlic powder around each of your bedrolls."

A grimace came over their faces; the idea of lots of garlic repelled them.

"Kidding! Just a little bit of Congo humor." Joseph and the Wantu broke out in laughter.

***

As they were laying out their bedrolls, Kyle naturally put his next to PoRue's without a thought about any taboos the Wantu might have about the two genders sleeping next to each other.

Nobody noticed — or if they did, it was of no concern, as they were too exhausted from the day's events, wondering and worrying.

"I'm getting to like this," PoRue whispered to Kyle. "It's like having a date without the pressure of sex."

Kyle just nodded and laughed.

While some were getting ready to sleep, others used their flashlights to look around the cave, checking for bats or any other creatures.

All at once came a crack and flash of light, followed by a muffled crunch. Everyone took out their flashlights to see.

"I can't believe it!" Lizzy exclaimed, shining her flashlight at the entrance to the cave. The lightning had struck just above the mouth and the rocks caved in, leaving a one-foot hole — just enough for them to breathe. The air could get in but they couldn't get out.

This was more than PoRue could stand.

"I *told you* we shouldn't go into another cave!" she yelled in exasperation.

Kyle looked at PoRue and the others with dread.

"We'll … we've got air … but what the hell are we going to do?" Walden asked no one in particular.

Joseph said, "That may keep big animals from getting to us during the night. It may be a blessing. In the jungle, you have to adapt. We will get a good night's sleep and we will find a way to dig out in the morning. Everyone, please, we'll be okay."

***

Joseph and Raku started waking everyone just after the sun came up. Even the small hole at the entrance allowed the sun to come shining in. The brigade made a small fire and started cooking breakfast.

Joseph told everyone to look in their packs for a folding shovel. The fallen debris was made up of small and medium-sized rocks, and they would be able to dig out, he assured them.

Shovels in hand and working side-by-side, they all started digging. The rocks and mud came away without much trouble, and was easier than any of them expected. All told, it took about an hour. Not everything was cleared, but enough so that the tallest — six-foot three-inch Sky — could get through, leaving space enough for the rest of them.

PoRue smiled. "Looks like we can get out without any more crisis."

She was right. Joseph gave everyone twenty minutes for breakfast, then ten minutes to get ready — meaning a thorough pack check and to make sure every item was easily accessible. This included a bathroom break, in the cave itself. The women would go a bit further in, and when done, the men would follow.

***

Joseph led. He went through the cave opening and stood for a minute, gazing at the forest. The sun was shining, greenery greeted him, birds were singing and blue duikers were grazing. It was a beautiful morning. He felt he was with a beautiful group of people whom he had come to love. He prayed that everyone would remain safe for the rest of the journey, and that they would see the white rhinos.

Sky saw Joseph praying and joined him in prayer for both their peoples and all beings.

With morning sun guiding the way, and most of the mud dried, the entourage was able to make it back to the jeep in less than two hours.

They would drive for half an hour, then stop at the trail for a fifteen-minute break, some snacks and *nukunia odela*. This would give them time to catch their breath before the half-hour walk to see the white rhinos.

"We're really going to see white rhinos today — I almost can't believe it!" Lizzy said.

"As long as we don't have to go into a cave to see them!" PoRue replied.

Walden told the teens how proud he was that they all showed concern and respect for the wildlife and environment, and especially for their hosts, the Wantu. He praised their keenness and quick action in moments of real danger and adversity.

They were all smiles, happy and excited to be part of a team that was helping. They were even more excited at the prospect of seeing white rhinos in the wild within the next two hours.

Back in the vehicles and on their way, they began to see more and more jungle wildlife the deeper in they went. There were more elephants, giraffes, hippopotamuses, varieties of deer and even occasional lions.

At last, they arrived at the trailhead.

"Your fifteen minutes start now," Joseph said. "Eat your MREs and check your packs to make sure everything is in place. Find a tree if you need to, but we will be leaving in fifteen minutes sharp. We don't want to challenge the rain gods."

Fifteen minutes later, the teens were ready.

"I know you're excited, but remember: safety must come first," Joseph told them. "Remember trail etiquette, looking up, down and all around. Snakes on the ground, predators above ground and in the trees. These are just examples. The kinds of dangerous wildlife are far too many to list, but you will be fine as long as you keep moving at a good pace and stay focused. Make sure you stay with the group."

Joseph led the way with Sky behind him and everyone else following. Raku watched the back of the pack. Naturally, PoRue and Kyle didn't care where they were on the line as long as they were together.

"I hope their romance works out," Sky whispered to Joseph, who seemed more attentive to what lay ahead.

So far so good. Joseph stopped momentarily to tell them they were about to arrive at a bit of a clearing and that once again there would be a wide stream below, a tributary of Congo River — and that this time of day the white rhinos should be there.

"Remember, if you're looking for wildlife, go to the water. The animals will eventually end up there."

Sure enough, as they came into the clearing, they could see ten adult white rhinos and three of their young close by. The rhinos were enjoying the water, submerging themselves on and off. They would rub against each other sideways or sometimes nose to nose. They were playing as well as anything that size can play. White rhinos grow to six feet high, thirteen feet long and can weigh over 5,000 pounds.

"Fear would be healthy when watching rhinos," Sky said, observing how some of the teens were overwhelmed by the animals' sheer size.

"That's true," Joseph agreed. "But that's not the most important thing about them. First, as long as you don't rile their young or invade their space, they are not going to attack you. You might call them the gentle giants. They have much better tempers than the black rhinos. More importantly, to the Wantu they are the most important species of the spirit world. They are known to bring inner peace and good luck to people who see them and treat them well and with respect. They are known to bring out the best of emotions in people. Third, despite their girth, they can run at thirty miles per hour, so running will do you no good if you do get them angry."

Sky said he could relate to the spirit world of the white rhinos, as his people thought well of all living things, and that a lot of their stories spoke well of many animals or wildlife.

Massimo, who'd never been around much wildlife, didn't know what to think of the spirit world and its connection to this one — including its wildlife — but he respected the thoughts of others in general and of the Wantu in particular, since they had become his friends.

"Did you see that one's eye?" Lizzy pointed.

"Which eye?" asked Janet.

"I was waiting to see who would see that first," Joseph said.

The largest rhino's left eye was bright orange.

"Really? Orange?" Kyle asked in amazement.

"We don't know what caused that, and nobody had ever seen a white rhino with an orange eye before, but our people named him Sun Eye because his eye blazes like the sun," Joseph recounted.

"Come on1 I've never taught anything like that in my class!" Walden sounded incredulous.

Joseph admitted that while he wanted them to see these white rhinos deep in the jungle, he also wanted them to see Sun Eye, because this white rhino was virtually one of a kind.

While everyone fixed on the orange eye, the professor started to speak on the rhinos' other qualities. He told them, for instance, that they didn't eat meat; rather, the white rhino ate leaves, short grass, plants and berries.

As if on cue, two white rhinos emerged from the water and started to graze on short grass and leaves.

"Look at that!" Sky pointed just as one of the rhinos stuck out its tongue and, in one grab, took in a bunch of berries on a branch.

Yet, despite their colossal size, these rhinos do have predators, the professor explained. Lions, tigers, hyenas and wild dogs will attack and pull them down as prey: in packs, these beasts can at-tack from the side or the back before the rhino is able to fight back or run off.

Dr. Walden also spoke about the white rhinos' personality, saying it had a stability, it was unusually limber for a thing of its size, and it was quiet, except when communicating with others of its kind.

The students didn't have to ask about the sounds, as they could hear the rhinos grunting and snorting. Sun Eye even made a whistling sound.

"Zoologists believe that the grunting and snorting — even the whistling — is the way they communicate with each other," Walden said.

The teens were going crazy taking photos and making videos on their phones.

"How do you top this? Cynthia asked, enthralled.

"You don't," answered Massimo, astounded by an aura of peaceful grace.

11

Politics, War and Peace

Early the following morning, Heart came running into the village yelling, "Joseph, Joseph, come quickly!"

Joseph appeared from his rondavel.

"We found the drug gang growing their crops about twenty miles to the north," Heart told Joseph, breathless, everybody within earshot listening.

"Let's load the troops into the jeeps. Be ready to go in ten minutes. How many were there?" Joseph asked.

"About fifteen, all with semiautomatics," Heart said.

Sky and Dr. Walden listened intently. Sky wanted to know how he could help. Walden did too, but needed to know that his entourage would be safe.

Joseph told Sky, who'd trained for this kind of action, that he would lead the third jeep, and Walden would have to stay behind with the teens and a few of the soldiers to protect them. The professor was glad to hear that the safety of the group was his top priority.

Instead of taking just twenty of their anti-poaching brigade, as they did on most patrols, they took sixty. This was serious business. They needed all the firepower they had.

"Did they see you?" Joseph asked Heart.

"Not as far as we can tell, but these drug runners are more organized and tech-savvy than the poachers, so they may have picked up our tracks after we left."

"I hope not," said Joseph, "the element of surprise always helps."

The Wantu soldiers knew what they had to do. They'd trained for this moment, never knowing at what point they would have to deal with this type of situation. The question was never whether, but when.

Their firearms and backpacks were always at the ready, just as they had the students practice in drills from the time they arrived.

Ten minutes later the jeeps took off, Joseph in the lead, Sky in the third jeep with the men he'd trained with, and Raku in the last jeep to guard the rear.

The soldiers checked their weapons and prayed along the way. They also checked through binoculars at all times, trying to spot any of the thugs before they were spotted.

The plan was to stop a mile or so from where the gang last was seen and spread out as they approached the illegal plants. They'd dealt with drug bandits before. They knew them to be hardened criminals who would kill without a second thought and come out in greater numbers if the Wantu failed to erase the problem now.

As soon as they stopped, the Wantu split into four groups of fifteen. Joseph would lead the group directly going in. Heart would lead the group from the left. The third group would approach from the right and Raku would lead the group from the back.

Joseph reminded them to be on the lookout for mines and booby traps. The soldiers moved through the woods slowly, and in just ten minutes they could see the gang through the trees. Eight were working in the fields. Six patrolled the perimeter, keeping an eye out for intruders but staying close to the field workers.

The soldiers knew there was at least one more — but where was he?

Not knowing the location of the missing worker could prove deadly during battle. Gunfire was unavoidable; the question now was containment, and how to minimize casualties. They were prepared and ready to start, but unsure how to finish.

First, bowmen would pick off the gangsters patrolling the perimeter. This would be done as silently as possible, because once the drug workers knew they were there, the gun battle would begin. That one of these scoundrels was nowhere in sight didn't help, but the tribesmen could think of no other way to approach it.

This had to be a coordinated attack. Joseph and Heart's groups split into pairs of smaller units to handle the six guards — and it had to be done with archers, all at once.

The Wantu warriors synchronized their movements. They knew the longer they waited, the more likely they were to be spotted. Things could turn deadly fast.

Joseph gave the signal and the arrows flew. The six on patrol were killed instantly. Even though the arrows silently *whooshed,* those working in the fields could see the patrols falling. They immediately raised their semiautomatics and started firing blindly into the tree line on all sides.

The Wantu arrows found two more targets, leaving six in the tribesmen's sights.

The gangsters dove to the ground, aimed high, and continued firing into the woods. By now the Wantu had stowed the bows and switched to firearms. The many trees and thick clusters of leaves made it hard to find targets; the gangsters couldn't even see where or at whom they were shooting.

Bullets nicked some of the soldiers on both sides of the fight in arms or legs, but not enough to endanger anyone's life.

During the exchange of fire one of the criminals snuck into the woods, where he spotted Heart's team. His plan was to sneak up on Heart from behind and kill him with his knife, then pick off Heart's men one by one.

Sky, though, was keeping an eye on Heart and saw what was about to happen. Almost as a reflex, Sky drew his bow and shot the man through the heart. He grunted and fell to the ground.

Heart whipped his head around and gasped. "You just saved my life! I'm so glad you joined our team! Now you're truly are one of us!"

Sky returned the compliment with a gentle smile.

The hooligans took shelter in a supply hut. Barricaded in, they used openings in the door and the small side windows to return fire. While bullets couldn't get to them, their own ability to shoot back was hampered too. It was unlikely that any of the Wantu would be hit.

Once they saw the thugs retreating, they were able to move in. Now the full complement of sixty soldiers, including Sky, were able to unload a barrage at the hut.

The semiautomatic fire hitting the structure was relentless and the six were pinned down inside, outgunned and deeply under-manned. They could hold out for a while, perhaps, but they knew they were alone and that no help was coming. They decided to surrender.

The leader held out a white flag in a last-ditch effort to save their lives. Joseph shouted to them in French that he would accept their surrender, and not knowing which tongue the men inside would understand, he had Sky yell the same in English.

The drug workers threw down their weapons in a pile in front of the hut and came out one by one, hands in the air. The Wantu approached slowly, in case the captured men were still armed.

Sure enough, one of the thugs drew a gun and shot a Wantu soldier, killing him. Heart quickly returned fire and killed the shooter. The rest of them dropped to their knees in total surrender.

The Wantu bound them, tying up their arms and hands.

"They killed Rakeem." Joseph frowned. "It will be tough telling his family."

He then approached their leader, asking for his name. "My name is Miguel. Why did you attack us?"

Joseph looked in disbelief. Plainly, Miguel did not understand that he was doing anything wrong.

Joseph felt he had to explain: the drugs they were growing hurt people. Not only that, they also have a terrible impact on the land and endanger the wildlife. Their drugs hurt the Great Creator's finest creations.

What Joseph deliberately left out, of course, was that this activity was too close to the Wantu's home — because if any of them escaped, they did not want them to know that the Wantu were here in the area.

"There were fifteen of you. Where is the missing one?" Joseph asked.

Miguel did a quick mental calculation and saw there was no future in not answering. "He went to the city for supplies. He won't be back for a couple of days."

Joseph instructed his men to take the prisoners to the jeeps. They had enough vehicles for one in each jeep to keep the prisoners apart.

Joseph thought about what to do with the prisoners once they returned to camp. These were not like poachers, who could be talked into changing their ways; rather, these were hardened criminals who would steal, rape, torture and kill if they believed it would help them in the slightest way. He couldn't simply let them go. If he did, they would certainly return and decimate the village.

Joseph asked Sky what they should do.

"It's a tough problem," Sky said, "because you want to show mercy, but there are times when the ways of your people are at stake. You would be hurting your people by showing grace to your enemies. You have to think about what's best for your loved ones."

Joseph agreed, but he also knew they were not barbarians and that he couldn't just assassinate his prisoners.

The entourage started home not knowing what they would do with the prisoners. Within three or so miles, Joseph spotted a body on the side of the road. The dead man had an arrow in his heart and a note attached to his shirt.

Everyone knew that Black Robin Hood had struck; this was his MO. Joseph asked Heart to examine the note while everyone kept watch for attackers.

Heart read the note aloud: *"You're welcome."* It was signed *BRH*.

BRH had taken down the drug desperado who'd gone ahead for supplies. The cartel workers in the city had no idea of their precise location, so Joseph and his people would not have to worry about any of this group returning.

***

As they continued the drive home, Heart introduced Sky to a fellow Wantu, Mobu, who had some special stories.

Unlike the rest of the Wantu, who had never left home except for supplies, Mobu had traveled into the major cities of central Africa to join protests against dictators and corruption. This took extra courage, because protesters in Congo were sure to face arrest, torture and beating.

Mobu not only wanted to keep the Wantu safe, but to address the injustices of his homeland. He wanted his homeland to change so that the Wantu and all those who lived in Congo would have a better way of life.

Ever a dreamer, Mobu was also an activist. Like other protesters, he was arrested and beaten. While some were killed or disappeared, he was lucky to live through a couple years of protests and about that same time in jail.

Lately his activism was more limited. He'd made his point and felt happy to leave the protests in other countries to those who live there. If he was going to die, he wanted it to be protecting his own people, their environment and way of life.

To Mobu, Congo was so immense that any one person or any one tribe were like ants in the forest: the deeper into the jungle, the less they were seen and felt; no one would find them. They would be as specks on the earth.

Even the part of the jungle where the Wantu lived seemed huge: the massive tracts of land, density of trees, the size of the elephants and rhinos, and the mighty Congo River.

Sky told Mobu that when they returned to the village, there were visiting teens from America who would love to hear his stories and learn from them.

"You must tell them during the community meal," Sky insisted.

"Gladly. We're all friends here," said Mobu. "As long as they don't steal my *nukunia odela*!"

Joseph smiled. "I know now what we're going to do with the prisoners," he said. "We can't kill them and we don't want to take them to our home or let them go back to theirs. We will send them somewhere they want to go so they won't want to return. If we were evil, we would sell them to slave traders, but we don't have the heart for that. So, we'll send them to Kinshasa."

***

"We'll split up into two groups," Joseph announced. "Most of you will return to camp, the others will come with me. We'll take these men directly into the city, so they won't know where our camp is, in case they do return. You can never be too careful."

12

Golden Cat and Invasion

The Wantu idea of a burial is like an Irish wake without the booze, in that they bury those who pass on and then have a party. But since the Wantu don't drink, their idea of a party is *nukunia odela* and sweet herbs as part of a community dinner.

The community dinner is like an extended family meal. There can be heated disagreements, but when the dinner is over, they remain committed to one another.

The following morning began with prayers, then the solemn burial of those lost in battle the previous day — in this case, Akeem.

Since the Wantu believe that everyone lives on in their ancestors, they weren't too sad; they also believe death is part of the cycle of life. To the Wantu the cycle of life should be not only respected, but revered.

Joseph presided over the ceremony. While some tribes would never invite outsiders into such a solemn rite, the Wantu encouraged it. They prayed for everyone, and their belief in inclusion was just that. Once they believe they can trust someone, that person is

219

considered a brother or sister. Joseph took Sky as an adopted brother, so he kept him near during the ceremony.

Heart was tasked with making Professor Walden and his teen-aged crew feel welcome here as well.

"We're honored, of course," Walden responded. "We have come to think of all of you as our new family. Your loss is our loss."

The Wantu sang during the burial, but the songs were different from what the visitors had previously heard. They sang in very low voices, and the songs were sad at some points and joyful at others, as this reflected the cycle of life: the high and low points in anyone's life.

Kyle and PoRue presented Joseph and the Wantu with flowers to place along the graves. The pair rose early to gather flowers from a nearby field. After all, it was something else they could do together.

"This is our custom, and we hope it's okay with you," Kyle told them.

Joseph smiled.

"A gift from you is like a gift from the Gods," Joseph responded. "I bet this means it will rain."

Massimo had a strange look on his face, as though he didn't understand. Janet also appeared perplexed. Kyle explained that many tribes believe that when it rains, it means a person's soul is coming back to the earth. Joseph nodded.

Cynthia's first response was to go to Joseph and give him a hug. Then she started hugging the other Wantu nearby. "This is another custom from America, and I find hugs help in time of need. You can never get enough hugs," she said.

Joseph told Walden that his children must make him proud. Joseph knew that these were not the professor's real children, but that the teens viewed him as their second dad since he worked so hard to keep them safe throughout this journey. Joseph could also plainly see that the teens believed in the mission.

Sky, who was soaking everything in, felt he was a stranger in a strange land. The Wantu were extraordinarily different from him, but so too were the Americans, although he felt a kinship with Kyle and PoRue as fellow Native Americans from the same area.

***

After the solemn burial ceremony concluded, Joseph announced that it was time to return to their joyous way of life. That meant time for the community meal, the *nukunia odela,* and singing and dancing in the happy Wantu way. The men prepared the fire and the women started cooking, all singing and swaying as they worked.

Raku was one of the first to offer a special prayer for Akeem, a prayer for his Wantu people and for all living things. He then gave thanks for recuperating from his injury.

Heart beat his hand gently across his heart as he prayed for Akeem and gave thanks to his people, and thanks as well for his enlightened visitors.

Sky talked about what it was like to live in harmony with two cultures. He spoke about how, growing up, he learned to treat his Hopi people as special, but he also learned to get along with White people as well as other non-Indians. He knew Indians, he said, who were mad at Whites and Whites who didn't like Indians. He considered this unhealthy. He thought all people should get along. Now that he had met the Wantu, he considered it important to accept them, and he was happy that the Wantu would listen to stories about his people and accept him.

Kyle said he suffered from some anti-Indian racism at the racetracks, but he had met far too many nice White and non-Indian people to stereotype any race or individual.

PoRue said she had seen too much conflict between Navajo and Hopi over land. She had seen this tear too many people apart. Yet she also had seen marriages between Navajos and Hopis that remained strong and enduring as long as the land issues did not come up. One reason she and Kyle got along so well, she told them, is because they both like all people.

Lizzy said that growing up in Seattle, being around people of so many different ethnicities, she never gave race a second thought.

Cynthia said that in the course of her studies, she learned that domestic violence impacts people of every kind. Bullies are found in people of all races and ethnicities, as are victims. "It just taught me that any people of any group can be good or bad. People are just people," she said.

Massimo shared that thanks to his dad's work in jewelry, his experience was quite different from that of his friends and the people with whom he grew up. He said that while the neighborhood was a mixture of Black and White, the jewelry business was mostly White. His dad, though, would talk about the Africans he'd met during his travels, about those who would go out of their way to help him, and about how some of the governments he dealt with there are corrupt, as are governments all over the globe. The only way in which they differ, he'd said, are in levels of brutality. "Like they say, absolute power corrupts absolutely," Massimo concluded. "That's regardless of color of the skin." Janet nodded, adding that her experiences were similar to his.

Joseph liked that the visitors, for different reasons, each believed that people of all groups have the ability to be good or bad.

***

Joseph looked at Sky and the rest of the visitors, then looked to the mountain in the distance. "You see that?"

"It's a beautiful mountain," Sky said.

The mountain was covered in green forest and granite boulders that stood in beautiful contrast. The sun was bouncing off the rocks and trees. "There's gold in those mountains," Joseph declared.

"Really! Gold. Has anyone claimed it?" Sky asked. Walden and the teens listened with new interest.

"Not that type of gold," Joseph replied. "There's the golden cat. You said you were interested in endangered species. The golden cat is unique and endangered. Do you want to see it?"

Joseph watched as the interest on the visitors' faces grew.

"Yes!" they all chimed at once.

Walden asked how the golden cat was unique. The teens moved closer to Joseph, straining to hear what he would say.

"It is quite a sight to behold, when you can see it," Joseph said. "It's nocturnal, like many types of cats, and it's small, as African cats go, about a meter long, although with a half-meter tail it seems much larger. But it has two unique qualities. It can jump ten feet in the air, often surprising birds flying above. The golden cat also eats colobus monkeys, catching them by surprise because the monkeys don't expect the golden cat to jump that high either.

"The second unique quality it possesses is that when it feels threatened, the golden cat will change colors, to either red or yellow.

"The golden cat is also related to the caracal, a slightly larger cat. The caracal, which is usually red, also changes its fur color when it feels in danger, to either gold or green. When it changes to gold it can easily be mistaken for the golden cat. Both of these cats have green eyes. The golden weighs no more than 16 kilos; the caracal can weigh up to 19."

Joseph told them that if they go high up into the mountain and camp out, they'd have a good chance to see these cats at night. Although they are shy and have not been seen by many, still they can be tracked, as Raku taught himself to do.

Dr. Walden was excited about the prospect, but wanted to hear from the teens first. Sky watched and listened intently.

"Of course, we all want to go," Kyle said. The others all nodded and smiled in agreement.

Joseph warned that they would have to climb from 900 meters to 3 kilometers, taking the better part of a day to get there.

"Any of you can back out and stay in camp," he made clear.

"I'm not staying in camp after all we've been through," Janet said.

"Let's just avoid the caves," PoRue suggested.

One by one, each gave Joseph their answer. It was unanimous: all were excited to go for another once-in-a-lifetime adventure. They had faced injury and the risk of death on some trips already, but they knew they didn't have many days left, and it might be a long time before they ever came back.

***

Joseph told them that the experience would be great, but also arduous: this would be a long hike into the mountains. They needed energy and to feel well rested, so he advised that they take an hour to eat, then another to check their gear, relieve themselves and do whatever else they needed to do.

"Two hours it is," Walden said.

"As long as there are no caves." PoRue sounded trepidatious.

The rest of the teens chuckled, but understood.

PoRue and Kyle were sitting together through the ceremony and everyone could see that their love for each other was strong. They seemed to be as one.

Massimo and Janet watched them with interest. They exchanged glances, but that was all. As for being a couple, each thought they were doing just fine.

Walden, while proud of all his students so far, remained nervous about any number of things that could go wrong. Frequently he would close his eyes and silently pray that each would arrive home safely.

"They'll be all right," Joseph assured him, trying to buoy his confidence. The teens, he said, knew what they were doing and would be carefully watched over by the Wantu.

Sky felt as though he was part of both groups, and at the same time part of neither. Part of both because he related to everyone; part of neither because his memory was incomplete. Who he was still had missing pieces, and he continued to wonder how he fit in — and with whom.

***

Two hours later the jeeps were ready to go.

As always, Joseph was in the lead and Raku at the tail end, in the last jeep, Sky in the jeep behind Joseph, and PoRue and Kyle not caring what vehicle they were in as long as they were in it together; the same went for Massimo and Janet.

The drive to the mountain would take about three hours. They would start their hike at the base and ascend twelve miles to the top, where they would camp.

Joseph explained that, with plenty of wildlife along the way, the golden cats would be closer to the top. Once they reached two kilometers they should keep their eyes out for the cats, even though their best chance of spotting them would be after dark, when they were camping.

The villagers, praying for their safe journey, waved to the group as they were leaving. The journey through the jungle began.

They left the village at nine in the morning and arrived at the base of the mountain right about noon. "Ten minutes," was all Joseph needed to say. Everyone knew that meant bathroom break and pack check, and to make sure the packs were comfortable on their shoulders.

Just as they were getting ready to begin the ascent, Joseph offered them one more piece of advice. "If you get too close to the golden cat or the caracal, there are two things you should know. First, don't run, because they will think you are prey, and you cannot outrun them. Second, you should know that the golden cat and caracal don't attack humans unless provoked, or," he emphasized, "if you turn your back on them. As long as you are facing them, they will not attack; just don't turn away," he stressed. "Remember, if you are walking away from these cats, walk backward for as long as you can."

"That seems odd," Massimo said.

"There is no logic to the jungle, only logic in knowing what goes on, how best to prepare for it and how to react," Joseph said.

For him, logic meant that they follow procedure at all times: he, Joseph, in front, Raku at the tail, and the soldiers among the teenagers to make sure no one got lost.

Like most in the jungle, the trail was a game track — narrow. The colobus monkeys were shrieking above them, a sign that the golden cats and caracals were somewhere near, since the monkeys are their principal diet.

They weren't on the trail more than five minutes when the switchbacks began.

"Really? Are you serious?" Lizzy asked, looking up at the mountain. It seemed tougher than any climb she'd ever done.

"Come on, we can do it!" Janet said.

Sky wanted to reassure Lizzy, so he told her that if she became too tired, he would gladly take her pack. Lizzy looked perplexed. "You're the one always telling everyone to smile," Sky reminded her.

"Okay, I will," she said reluctantly.

The group started making its way slowly up the mountain. Joseph told them to pace themselves, letting everyone know that no one had to rush and that they would all keep an eye on one another to see if anyone needed help along the way.

Joseph also emphasized that no one should ever be left alone on this desolate trail, so everyone had a trail buddy to watch them, including the soldiers. They didn't want poachers or drug hoodlums picking them off one by one, or kidnapping anyone — or any animals dragging them off.

The Wantu soldiers carried semiautomatics along with their packs, while the visitors' packs included guns, knives, first aid, food and water.

They hiked at a steady two miles per hour, even with stopping to catch their breath as they climbed ever higher. The trees became more spread out with each mile they climbed.

Even with stopping for snacks, the hike would take eight hours. They would arrive at the campground on the peak at around 8pm. At this time of year, it remained light until nine, so they would have about an hour to set up their tents and light the fires needed for dinner.

Walden noticed how everything changed as they rose. The plants and trees were different at each altitude. The birds changed too, with parrots and songbirds more numerous lower down and eagles and hawks more plentiful here, soaring off the cliffs. They had left the giraffes, zebras and most of the other wildlife behind them. Cats of various sizes and bears were more likely seen near the top.

***

Sky moved up and down the line more than anyone else during the hike, continually checking on the teens to make sure everyone was all right. He was concerned about the onset of altitude sickness and whether the hike was getting to be too much for any of them.

They appreciated his concern, but so far all were holding their own in terms of keeping up. Walden was able to both keep up with the pace and watch the teens, but checking each one individually was more than he could physically handle, so he was happy to have Sky's help.

Joseph too was concerned about everyone, including his soldiers, but he saw that Sky had the situation in hand and was content to let Sky do his volunteer job.

As they went up, the views became more stunning, especially of the lowland forest below. At first, they could see animals grazing in the distance, but as they rose higher the wildlife became smaller and smaller; soon they were no more than little dots, then disappeared out of sight.

***

They arrived at the campground on the peak right on time. As the hikers dropped their packs, Joseph told them they would have five minutes to rest, then they would need to set up their tents before dark. During their short break Raku would talk to them.

"I need to tell you two things," Raku said. "But before I do, I need to ask you one question: What do you think we like best about Americans?"

The group members looked perplexed at first, then some volunteered their answers. "Our money?" Massimo kidded. Clearly, that couldn't possibly be the most important asset in the jungle.

"Our smiles?" asked Lizzy.

"The way our cultures relate to yours?" PoRue thought she had it.

They all fell silent, waiting for Raku's answer.

"Marshmallows," Raku said, half serious. "Some of the Americans who came here years ago brought marshmallows, and our people love them. There is nothing like roasted marshmallows. So, the soldiers *all* brought marshmallows in their packs so everyone can roast them over the campfires."

This brought a round of applause.

"The second thing is, if you want to see the golden cats and the caracals, then pitch your tents quietly." Raku brought his voice low. "The cats are curious, so they will see the campfires and come to the edge of the camp to watch us. They never come into camp, but they will come close. So, then you'll have a chance to see them. Watch the bushes and you'll see them move, but the first thing you'll notice is their bright green eyes. The eyes really stand out, especially in the dark."

Lizzy asked if she *didn't* see the cats and her back was toward them; would the cats attack?

"No," Heart chimed in. "They only attack if someone first makes eye contact and *then* turns their back. Just the way of the jungle."

Walden assured Joseph and his men that the teens would comply, which the Wantu already knew, since the group had followed directions closely from the moment they arrived. In their brief time here, the teens saw how deadly the jungle can be, and had come to respect the Wantu, and wanted to show that in any way they could.

"I need to help PoRue with her tent," Kyle announced, to everyone's amusement. "I'll help Janet with hers," echoed Massimo.

Before anyone else had a chance to volunteer, Sky offered to help any others who needed assistance setting up their tent.

The Wantu soldiers then lit the campfires and started cooking dinner, breaking out the *nukunia odela* and marshmallows.

***

PoRue was helping Kyle with the stakes when she nudged him, using her head to point to the bushes to the left.

Kyle spotted the staring green eyes. They both stopped. The golden cat was about fifteen feet away, its golden fur shining in the moonlight. The cat moved silently, with confidence and deliberation, as though greeting them while showing off.

The others noticed the couple watching and started watching too. The golden cat sashayed back into the night.

"That was so cool!" PoRue and Kyle *oohed* at the same time.

Raku told them that was only the beginning of what they would see that night. Since these animals are nocturnal, they could stay up as long as they wanted to watch the wild cats. The good news, he added, is that they would be allowed to sleep in.

This brought a quiet cheer — so as not to scare the cats off.

By now the Wantu soldiers had the fires roaring. Soon everyone had their tents up. They all huddled around the campfire as they started on dinner, drinking *nukunia odela* and roasting their marshmallows.

They used their otherwise useless phones to take photos, knowing that family and friends would have a hard time believing this.

As the night wore on, they heard more bushes moving and saw more green eyes observing them. One of the golden cats moved into the open and just laid down, but it never stopped watching them.

The evening air was cool, and they wrapped up in small blankets from their packs, PoRue and Kyle together. No one commented.

Massimo didn't have the environmental background the others did, but he was mesmerized watching the golden cats coming and going through the night. "This is amazing! They're so beautiful, it's almost like they're big house cats and I just want to approach them, but I'm guessing that wouldn't go well."

Janet let out a happy sigh. "The cat is beautiful, but I'm not getting any closer and neither should you," she told him.

Heart told them that if they approached, the caracal would run off before they got close, but if cornered it most certainly would attack. The only other time a cat might attack, he said, is if it were rabid.

Sky too was smitten with the golden cats and caracals, he'd never seen anything like them. He found rare beauty in watching the golden cat glow with the moonlight hitting just right. The cats would pop in and out of the nearby forest, ever curious about the visiting humans; they too wanted to watch.

Walden kept an eye out, quietly taking notes so he could tell his students all he'd seen on this most recent African adventure. The teens stayed quiet as they watched the cats, but they also watched each other's faces in silent communication.

As the sun started to rise, the cats came around less and less, till they vanished altogether. One by one the teenagers slid into their tents and faded off to sleep.

Joseph let everyone sleep till noon. Then he had the soldiers and Sky wake the group, telling them that food would be ready in twenty minutes and to be fully prepared to hike down the mountain in one hour, sharp.

Breakfast was simple: eggs and wild-pig bacon to go with their coffee and *nukunia odela*. Some chose to eat first, others broke down their tents and secured their packs. "We enjoy our morning coffee on the rez too," Sky recalled.

"Sure do," Kyle added. "We can talk about the day ahead."

"If I can make it to Starbucks, it's even better," PoRue chimed in.

***

Kyle was quick to take down his tent so he could help petite PoRue with hers. He was busy on one side of her tent when she let out a pained yelp from the other. He came running, and Sky was right there too, the others not far behind.

PoRue had been bitten by a puff adder, one of the deadliest snakes in Africa. This gray-white snake is one of the largest, with some reported over five feet long.

The adder's principal defense is camouflage, so people don't usually see it. When they do, it can often be too late. The snake is fast and hits hard, with a force of impact known to penetrate soft leather. Avoiding this adder isn't helped by its habit of basking near footpaths and remaining quiet when approached. As for its strike, poor PoRue could not have seen it coming.

Add to this that the adder isn't usually found this high. Joseph and the Wantu had the hikers looking out for snakes lower down, not necessarily here on the peak.

Sky knew how to handle snakes from ceremonies, and so he grabbed it from behind and snapped its neck. The spooky part was that its head started going off in one direction while its writh-ing body moved in another, until both collapsed and died.

"That's creepy." Lizzy shuddered, along with the others.

"This will be in my nightmares," Janet said.

Heart attended to PoRue's wound. Kyle was shaking with fear that he might lose her, but Heart knew precisely what to do.

By this time the pain had set in. Heart told her she was lucky: fortunately, the bite did not go in deeply, so she was spared the usual amount of venom, very often lethal if not treated right away.

Heart had the soldiers retrieve his pack. He took out a red poultice.

"Non-Africans don't know how to deal with snakebites; even most tribes here do not. But some time ago we discovered that this flower, found in the bush, is perfect for just this type of in-jury," he said while applying the salve.

Heart assured PoRue that the rosy poultice would give her quick relief. She would be okay for the hike down, he said, but she wouldn't be able to carry her pack. She could carry a bottle of water and that would be it. They would split the items in her pack among her fellow hikers.

"That's fine," Kyle said as the other teens nodded. They all huddled around PoRue, but Walden told them to give her room so she wouldn't feel uncomfortable and anxious.

"I'm not leaving her side," Kyle insisted.

"Nobody expects you to. I'd be disappointed if you said any-thing different," said Heart.

PoRue was shaking from the pain and trauma. Tears fell, but Heart's assurance began to sink in. She steadied herself.

"Help me up," she said, looking at Kyle.

Kyle pulled her up and watched for a minute to make sure she was stable enough to stand on her own and walk.

PoRue smiled with the realization that she would make it. She was even happier when she saw that she could stand on her own and that the poultice had relieved her pain.

"Get me to breakfast!" she urged.

"Not so fast!" Kyle said, embracing her. "You gave me the scare of my life. I want to have you around for a long, long time."

Kyle gently led her to a seat the Wantu set for her by the breakfast area. Everyone breathed easier when they saw she'd be okay.

"There is something to be said for forest medicine," Heart said.

The soldiers started singing softly to help PoRue feel at peace. They wanted the music to lift her spirits, but they also knew that she was sore and might not appreciate anything loud.

PoRue most certainly appreciated it.

The group fell to eating and talking. The coffee was a nice wake-up and the *nukunia odela* a joy. Though served with almost every meal, it never got dull because it was so invigorating.

"We have nothing to match this juice in America," Massimo declared. "We have energy and juice drinks, but nothing that leaves everyone as refreshed as this."

Joseph took a moment to address the group, to say he was glad PoRue was all right and that everything was okay. The snake-bite incident set them back an hour, which was no big deal, but they had to be ready to go soon.

Everyone by now had learned the drill and were ready on time. The line was the same going down, Joseph leading, Sky behind, Raku at the tail and the soldiers among the teens.

The group moved at a quick, steady pace down the mountain, stopping every half hour for five minutes or so to down a few energy bars or whatever they could to keep going.

Four hours in, halfway down the mountain, Joseph called everyone to a halt, his gaze fixed on the forest below.

"I see what you see," Sky said.

Joseph put a finger to his lips, motioning everyone to be quiet. Below, something was moving through the trees. It wasn't animals.

"We'll keep moving," he whispered, "but very slow for now. When I stop, everybody else stop, understood?"

Everyone nodded.

They moved about a quarter of a mile further down when Joseph spotted a note waiting for them.

He picked it up and read it to himself.

"Give us the one who fell from the sky and we will leave the rest of you alone," it read.

He folded the note and put it in his pocket without telling the others what it said. "They know we are here and they plan to attack."

The Wantu live life as a collective, meaning that everyone in the tribe has equal importance. They would never let any of their people be taken by anyone who would hurt them. The Wantu had adopted Sky into their tribe, so they were not about to turn him over to a gang that would surely kill him.

Joseph also knew that these hoodlums were no match for them in their forest.

He turned to the visitors and told them never to speak about what they were about to witness. He had their attention. No one moved.

He then told Raku to do his duty.

Raku reached into his backpack and took out a flute that had been folded so it was easier to carry. He unfolded it and blew into it, making a high-pitched whistle. He did this repeatedly, and each time the whistle grew louder.

Pretty soon a rumbling began in the forest below. The ground and the mountain all began to shake. With each passing second the rumbling grew louder, and the shaking harder.

A stampede.

Now they could plainly see the herds of elephants stampeding through the jungle. Unusual behavior for elephants, which is what made the moment so unique. They ravaged it, crushing everything in their path. Trees fell. They could hear the guns of the criminals, but not for long: too many animals were moving too fast. The outlaws had no time to respond.

The visitors watched in awe and no small horror as the drama unfolded before their eyes. The Wantu had done this at other times and places, when needed for survival. Even so it was incredible to watch, no matter how often they'd seen it.

"Why don't you want us ever to speak of this?" Massimo wanted to know.

"Because we don't want our enemies to know we have this power," Joseph answered bluntly. "Also, some here will think of this as bad magic, and they may want to take revenge."

"On our rez there are many things we don't talk about," said Sky. "Many things we keep secret. Many things we keep to ourselves."

"No one back home would believe it anyway," Walden said.

"We'll start down the mountain, but some of them may have survived, so be on the lookout, and alert us if you see anything even remotely suspicious," Joseph said.

It was four more hours back to the vehicles. The next two were uneventful, except for everyone's being on edge. Then they came around a corner and found three bodies pierced with arrows.

Now there are three less, read the note, signed *BRH*.

Joseph told the group that if Black Robin Hood made it up this far, there were no other criminals on the mountain now, and that the stampede below made survivors there unlikely.

"We should be safe from this point on, but we need to be careful, always," Joseph warned.

13

Coming Home

Down from the mountain at last, they returned to their jeeps and their jaws dropped.

One vehicle was totally burned out. The other jeeps had their tires slashed, including all the spares.

Joseph looked a little surprised, but wanted everybody composed. "You always learn to expect the unexpected in the jungle," he told them evenly.

Lizzy started crying. "This is too much! W-what are we going to do?" she whimpered.

Massimo was ruffled, but didn't want anyone to break down or panic. He went to Lizzy and gave her a hug, telling her it would be okay.

"Try to keep it together." Joseph spoke calmly. "We will be fine."

Kyle went over to one of the jeeps and rubbed his hand across the hood. "This is wrong on so many levels."

PoRue followed Kyle over to the jeep — clearly upset, though not falling apart. "This is just disturbing," she agreed.

Cynthia sat down on the ground and simply stared, to see what the group would do next.

Sky went to the jeeps and examined each one carefully.

Joseph, Raku, Heart and the soldiers surveyed the nearby woods. They were watching for any kind of movement. Nothing. Surely if any of the enemy survived, they would have attacked by now.

Joseph went over to the vehicles to check the locked boxes. The attackers hadn't bothered with them.

"This is good," he said. "There is water, energy bars, lunch meat and bread in the fireproof boxes. Everybody put some in your backpacks."

By now it was 8:30pm and only half an hour of light remained.

Raku told everyone that a good spot to camp was within fifteen minutes' walk. Just enough time to arrive and get the tents up before dark.

Joseph unlocked the boxes in the all jeeps except one — the burned-out vehicle where the box burned so hot that it too went up in the fire.

"Let's hustle to the campground and get everything set up. Then we'll eat and get to sleep. We will have a long walk out in the morning," he said.

Everyone grabbed their water and rations from the boxes in the jeeps.

Apparently, the attackers thought they would win the battle, and if there did happen to be any survivors, they wouldn't be able to drive out. Since none of the attackers apparently survived, it just meant a long walk back.

Raku led. The road to the campground was wide enough for them to go in pairs, threes or no particular order.

Sky took the rear to keep an eye out for anything coming from behind. Joseph, along with the soldiers and Dr. Walden, kept an eye out for anything else.

After walking for ten minutes Raku stopped to indicate a new direction, to the right. Sure enough, they could see a small game trail leading into the woods. A five-minute walk brought them into a small open meadow, where a campfire once had been. Clearly it had not been used for some time.

"As you can see, this is far enough off the beaten track that no one will find it unless they knew where it is or happen upon it," Raku said.

With not much daylight left, Joseph told everyone to get their tents up quickly. The soldiers lit the campfires and helped the teens with their tents, with help from Sky and Heart.

"Yes, we have more marshmallows!" Raku said.

That brought smiles but not much cheering; the teens knew they had to get their tents up fast, eat and get to sleep early. The long walk back to the village tomorrow promised to be a grind.

Once the tents were up, one by one they moved over to the campfire.

"This has been one helluva trip!" Massimo said to all.

"I was concerned about my safety — everybody's safety — but I believe the worst is behind us," Lizzy said.

"Let's keep everything positive," Janet chimed in.

Joseph agreed with both statements, reminding them to keep a sharp eye out, for anything from poachers to stampeding elephants.

"Just when I was starting to think positive!" Lizzy sighed.

***

Heart announced dinner as the soldiers handed out the *nuku-nia odela* and told them the armadillo burgers soon would be ready. The visitors' eyes widened, but if the Wantu were serving it, they would at least give it a try.

The Wantu started a cheerful song. Though the visitors couldn't understand the words, they knew it was upbeat. "What are you singing?" Cynthia asked no one in particular.

Heart replied that it was a joyous song about surviving another day, about their people surviving another day; it also was a prayer for their people, their visitors, for everybody and all living things.

"Can't argue with that," Massimo said through a mouthful of armadillo.

The Wantu swayed as they sang. The visitors couldn't help but join in. Nobody cared if anyone sang off-key — they were singing as one, about community.

"Why do you sing?" Janet asked.

"Because it's a joyous way to live and express yourself," Joseph answered.

It certainly was a joy-filled night. The fun went on for about another hour, and by then all knew the protocol. Everyone took a few more bites, drank a few more sips, and headed off to their tents.

***

Joseph directed the soldiers to wake everyone as the sun was rising. It was just about 5am, but the Wantu lived by sunrise and sunset, so time of day didn't mean much to them.

Time became meaningful when they had somewhere to be. In this case Joseph knew the hike would take nine hours back to the village, so he wanted everyone ready to go. Fifteen minutes, as usual, for the tents, and half an hour for breakfast. Forty-five minutes all told to be ready, including all the other checks.

Walden promised Joseph that everyone would be ready on time.

Lizzy groaned, but nodded along with the rest.

"You can do it," Janet said.

"It'll be a walk in the park," Kyle said cheerily, trying to keep upbeat. PoRue had come to love that about him, and returned a beautiful smile.

"Oh, something *has* to happen between here and the village," Massimo predicted.

"Don't be so cynical. It could be something good!" Cynthia said with hope.

Sky had been watching and carefully listening. "Come on, you guys," he said. "You've been through a lot and you're resilient. Whatever the jungle throws at you on the way back, you should be able to handle. It's not like any of you are alone. You have soldiers to protect you, and you have the good jungle spirits to protect you."

"I didn't think of it like that, I'm just *tired*," Lizzy said.

"We all are, but we must persevere and stay as positive as we can," Kyle said.

"That's what I'm talking about," said Janet.

"We've come this far and this is where we begin the first part of our journey home," Massimo pointed out. "But we're not only protected by soldiers, we're with our friends, and I wouldn't give this back for anything in the world."

***

Sky resumed helping the teens with their packs, making sure they were in order and that all items within were accessible.

Joseph reassured the visitors. "The only difference between you and the soldiers is that soldiers don't need a pep talk," he said. The teens looked at him as though he were serious, then realized he was joking.

Lizzy felt better after gulping down some *nukunia odela* and breakfast. Everyone felt better after eating. The packs were on and they were ready to go.

All they had to do, Joseph told them, was follow the road: he would lead, with Raku at the tail to check for any danger. The road was wide, they could walk two abreast, meaning Heart, Walden and the teens on one side and the soldiers on the other.

As they set out, the teens started singing in English, and before long the soldiers learned the words and joined in. Then the Wantu would sing in French and the teens would join in as well as they could, mimicking the dialect.

The group was upbeat and moving at a nice even pace for the first hour.

The breeze was slight, not enough to move the trees or bushes much. While the trees barely moved, the bushes rustled, more than one would think the breeze would allow. From the look and the sound of it, it was too small to be anything human and certainly no large animal, but it had to be more than one.

"Look up ahead, on the road," Sky said.

Everyone could see something massive red and brown moving across the road. Joseph groaned.

"It's strange!" PoRue exclaimed. "I want to go closer!"

Joseph held up his hand for them to stop. "That would be unwise. Those are driver ants, and this is their annual migration. Billions of them migrate from inland to the river. They're called that because they keep driving, keep moving, regardless of anything in their path. If they get on you, they will cause rashes; if too many get on you, they will eat at you until you fall and then they will devour you. If any get in your eyes you will quickly go blind. You have to wash it out with alcohol right away."

PoRue's eyes were bulging with the thought of getting ants in her eyes. "I think I'll leave them alone!" she said.

"Gross!" said Cynthia.

"I plan to keep my distance," said Lizzy.

Massimo said his father never told him any stories about driver ants. "He must not have seen them, because I know he'd have told me if he did," he said.

While he'd seen plenty of weird insects, including ants, on the reservation, Kyle admitted that he'd never before heard of anything like this.

Janet didn't say a thing, but she pulled down her hiking hat as close to her eyes as possible.

The reason they could barely see the ants from a distance was because they were so individually tiny. That they could see them at all is because there were so many. Army ants move in thousands; driver ants make their way with millions.

Joseph told the group not to worry: they were not in the path of the migration. He directed that they put down their packs and rest for fifteen minutes, and the ants would pass in that time. Once they started walking again, they should keep their eyes peeled for any lingering ants.

Once they got going, Joseph assured them that the soldiers would keep an eye out for ants, and warned them against going off for a bathroom break till they were well clear of the danger. Anyone needing to go, he said, should do it in the road behind them. The teenagers looked too scared to try it.

"I think I speak for the group when I say we'll hold it," Kyle told Joseph.

PoRue grabbed his arm. "I'm not doing anything until they pass!" she said with a shudder.

***

The next two hours breezed by. The group was quieter, on the lookout for ants and other dangers, but all they saw were monkeys and birds in the trees, and heard elephants in the distance.

Joseph raised his hand once more for everyone to halt. "What is odd right now?" he asked.

Walden, Sky and the other visitors didn't have a clue. Joseph, Raku and the soldiers were well aware of the oddity. "Raise your guns, but don't be quick to fire," Joseph told them.

The professor wondered what they were seeing. Then he knew: the trees and bushes had been blowing in a gentle breeze, and now they had stopped, almost as though they were frozen.

Raku said they probably had them surrounded by now.

"Who's *they?*" Massimo asked.

"The Cantu pygmies," Raku responded. "They have a spirit about them that quiets the trees and bushes, and you don't know it till it's too late; we're not their enemies, so it should not be a problem."

Sure enough, a Cantu warrior appeared from the woods as if out of nowhere. To anyone unfamiliar with the Cantu, here was a strange sight indeed: a tiny warrior, three feet tall, thin, with battle paint over his eyes.

Some might laugh, but the Wantu knew better. The Cantu were well known fighters, having won battles against the fiercest poachers and drug lords. Being perennially underestimated worked to their advantage. They also had trained themselves in martial arts and acrobatics. They would attack from below *and* above, swinging down from the trees to injure opponents. So, they were difficult to catch or strike.

"Chief Kyombo, how can I help you today?" Joseph asked in Cantu. Joseph looked at Heart, who knew he had to translate so everyone else in the entourage would understand.

"Great leader, you can help us today the way you always have: by working together?" The chief replied in Cantu: "There are poachers about ten minutes from here. We are always stronger and always do better when we work together. We saw you were in the area and assumed you would want to help."

"You know we are concerned about the poachers, and yes, we are stronger when we work together. We *should* work together," Joseph responded. "As you can see, we have visitors and they are not trained in battle, so we have to keep them safe while we engage."

"So be it," said the chief. "Just up this trail is a cave that no one knows about. We can leave them there while we do what we have to do."

"Oh no, not another cave!" PoRue cried in despair. Heart interpreted that for the chief.

"What's wrong with her?" Chief Kyombo asked once he knew what she was saying. "Does she have a fear of caves?"

"It's more about her recent experience, but later. I imagine time is short," Joseph responded. Chief Kyombo motioned for everyone to follow him.

Single file they went, Joseph behind the chief, Raku at the tail, as usual.

Chief Kyombo led them to the cave, where they left the professor and his group, along with some soldiers for protection. The rest of the party followed the Cantu up to the highest point on a nearby hill.

"The poachers don't know that we have seen them — and since this place is remote, they feel safe enough to take their time. They've killed four elephants and are cutting the tusks off with saws, which is going to take them a little while, but we have to act soon," said the chief.

Joseph, Heart and Sky looked down. Out in a huge meadow, they could see the poachers hard at work, sawing off the tusks. Eight poachers working on four dead elephants, the jungle forest right behind them.

Enclosing the meadow were two small hills with a poacher on each as lookouts. Neither could see as far up as the pygmy chief had taken the Wantu soldiers.

On a smaller hill just below them, one more poacher stood guard.

"What's the plan?" Joseph asked in Cantu.

Chief Kyombo said they had to take care of the lookouts first — that's where they needed the most help. Once that was done, he said, the rest of the poachers would not be a problem. On this last point, the chief further clarified that while easy to shoot, he didn't want to just assassinate the poachers.

"The ants are migrating in the forest behind them. The poachers don't know that. It will be easier for them to retreat into the forest than to scale the surrounding hills after we attack. We've set traps for them deep in the forest: ropes attached to trees that are hidden under the brush. When the poachers fall, the ants will find them, and we will capture what's left of them."

At that point, said the chief, they would send the poachers off to a prison far away, where they would have no chance of returning.

"I like the plan," said Joseph.

"It's genius," Kyle chimed in.

The lookouts, though, were another story. If they survived to make enough noise, a gun battle would be sure to erupt, and a lot more people on both sides would be killed.

The Wantu and Cantu agreed: minimize the causalities of the enemy, but not at the expense of their own.

The famed Wantu archers had no problem taking out the three lookouts. They were able to get within 300 feet without being spotted. Then the arrows flew, hitting them right in the heart. It was quick, silent and deadly.

Meanwhile the Cantu had taken their place on the hill overlooking the meadow with their firearms. The Wantu joined them, bows ready. The plan was to shoot in front of the poachers, chasing them back into the forest.

On the pygmy chief's signal, the bullets and arrows rained down — but instead of retreating, the poachers let loose with their semiautomatics, firing blindly in all directions and advancing. The Cantu, having no other choice, returned fire, killing three of them.

The other five poachers, though, ran into the forest, continuing to fire away as they fled. Then, when they were out of sight, the shooting stopped and everything fell silent.

Chief Kyombo and Joseph together agreed to track the remaining five. None could be allowed to escape. Their vehicles, now abandoned, were parked right next to the dead elephants. The thieves had not anticipated a gunfight.

***

Not far into the forest in back of the meadow, the trackers found their first poacher. Sure enough, he had tripped on the trap and the ants devoured him.

Having seen their comrade fall, the other poachers, aware of traps, became a bit more careful, but then a second one fell further up. The trackers found this one still alive, with rashes all over, and one had got into his right eye. Heart cleaned out his eye and they took him captive. Two down, three to go.

Further up the trail they heard gunfire. It was the poachers' way of saying they were armed and that to apprehend them would be dangerous. Yet the trackers knew if they let them go, the enemy would return in greater numbers.

They also knew that in a couple of miles, the poachers would run out of space. Soon they would come to a very steep cliff with the far below. Even if they could descend, they would find crocodiles and other deadly animals, and crossing the river would be impossible. The Congo was too wide, deep and fast to get across without drowning.

They knew the poachers, once they found out, would have to take a stand or surrender. The odds were 35 to three, but the poachers didn't know that, and the soldiers didn't want to take casualties.

They worried that the enemy would lie in wait and start spraying them with gunfire or climb into trees and shoot them from above.

Surprisingly, the poachers didn't do either. When they reached the cliff and saw they could go no further, the leader of the three came up with an idea: they would set the jungle on fire, and in the commotion move past their trackers and escape to wherever they could. This, they figured, was their only hope.

But when they lit the fire, the wind rose from the opposite direction. The fire surrounded them and they had nowhere to go. They jumped off the cliffs to their deaths.

Now the fire started to spread — and quickly — toward the soldiers. First, they saw smoke. Minutes later they could see the flames. They knew they had to get out of there.

Chief Kyombo and Joseph ordered everyone out as fast as they could run. They made it back to the meadow in short order, out of breath, but safe. The fire, they knew, wouldn't move through the meadow with anything near the same speed as in the jungle, giving them time to recuperate.

After a couple of minutes, they headed to the cave, keeping ahead of the fire. They reached the cave and announced to everyone that they would have to camp there overnight to avoid perishing in the inferno. The boulders above and below them wouldn't burn, so the fire would not be able to enter. Here, in the cave, they would be safe.

***

Terrified by the cave, PoRue couldn't stop talking, and rocking. It was the only way to deal with her fear, and it was driving the rest of them crazy. When the Wantu and Cantu parties showed up, the teens at first were overjoyed, then concerned that a fire was consuming the jungle.

"Great to see you," Massimo said, somewhat unnerved at the sight of two bound prisoners. "Maybe now PoRue will stop babbling."

"What do you mean?" Joseph asked.

Walden explained about her fear of caves. He had tried to comfort the distressed PoRue, but it only partially worked. The other teens did what they could, with similar results.

Janet gave her frequent hugs, but these kept her calm only minutes at a time.

PoRue, for her part, was glad to see that they got back safely. Then she just smiled, curled up and at last went to sleep.

Those who stayed behind had dozens of questions. After getting settled, Joseph and Sky told the group precisely what had transpired. Now all were looking out the cave entrance, some with eyes agog, at the spreading fire.

Joseph immediately directed his soldiers to start preparing the meal, for two reasons: to take their minds off the wildfire, and so everyone could eat before going to sleep. Come morning, he told them, they had five hours of walking to get back to their village, assuming no unforeseen delays.

The teenagers were beginning to look frazzled. A good hot meal would help. As for the unforeseen in the jungle, well, that would have to take care of itself for now.

Joseph told them life in the jungle came with good and bad streaks. Sometimes they would go for months on end without anything eventful. Those times were good, as they could go about their peaceful ways unruffled, undisturbed. Then there were those other times, when they would have to deal with poachers, other intruders, problems with wildlife or floods — or fires.

"Most of the time life is good." He paused. "But often, it can be challenging."

***

Raku was first to be awakened by the sun. He started waking the other guards, so they could get the coffee and breakfast going. Raku was also first to look below. He could see that most of the area had been burned out by the fire. As the others woke, they too came over to see the destruction. It was devastating.

The teenagers looked down in depressed amazement, bordering on shock.

Sky recalled seeing televised wildfires and seeing them frequently in the news, but nothing like this, and never firsthand. He looked utterly bewildered.

Kyle, eyes fixed on what had happened below, remarked about the frequency of fires on his reservation, and that the fires were increasing in ferocity.

Joseph told them not to stare too long and not to dwell on it. He said fire was the Great Creator's way of managing the jungle, regardless of whether it was man-made or caused by lightning.

"Breakfast is ready. Eat, drink and be prepared to get going. We have a five-hour walk out, and that's assuming we can even find the trail," Joseph said.

260

Raku smiled. "I brought my GPS!" he said.

While the Wantu worked hard to retain their tribal ways, they knew that to survive they had to modernize equipment. Sometimes GPS is exactly what was needed.

After breakfast and backpack protocol, they marched into the fire-ravaged landscape with Raku leading the way, and within half an hour they found what was left of the trail. The trees that remained standing looked barbecued, and the odor of smoke was strong.

Raku explained that they wanted to get through this as quickly as possible. First, without trees, branches or leaves to block the sun, it would be much hotter; and second, they did not want to inhale the smoke any longer than they had to.

"With your packs and the considerable distance left to go, you cannot run. So just go at your steady pace, but continue to keep your eyes peeled: watch straight ahead and to both sides. Not much need to look up, the trees are all burned out. The guards will be watching from the back."

Everyone walked quietly without much talk, concerned about just getting through. After an hour or so, they started to notice some of the trees were not fully burned, and some of the birds and monkeys had returned.

"This is good," Raku said. "This shows that sometime soon we will be able to see where the fire stopped."

The further they walked, the more trees they saw alive and the more monkeys and birds appeared. About half an hour later, a jeep was heading toward them on the narrow, burned-out trail. "That's one of ours," Raku said, relieved. Everyone cheered.

A jeep with four Wantu soldiers pulled up. Speaking in French, the driver explained that when their lookouts saw the fire, they sent out search parties. The roads, he said, were slow-going. The rains from last night saved the village from burning, just as they were ready to evacuate.

"I have never been so happy to see you, Abu, and hear the good news," Joseph told his fellow tribesman.

"That's what you taught us we are all about," Abu replied.

***

There were hugs of happiness all around. The Wantu and Cantu were thrilled because, by some miracle, both their villages had been saved. The Cantu village was even farther away, but in the jungle, there's no telling what can happen with a fire; that they too were saved was just as miraculous.

The teens were happy because now they knew they would make it back to the village safely — and with jeeps, it would be that much quicker.

One teen could fit in Abu's jeep to go back to the village; a convoy would return for the others. Lizzy raised her hand. "Okay, it's you!" Abu said.

Lizzy clapped her hands in joy and climbed into the jeep at once.

"That's the fastest I've seen her move the entire trip!" Massimo murmered.

"Let her go. We're tougher," said Janet.

Joseph said the group would keep on walking, to save fuel and distance traveled when the entourage came back. Walking also would get them that much closer to home.

Abu's jeep slowly turned around on the burned-out road. Just as the jeep took off in one direction, from the other direction Black Robin Hood came strolling into camp, seemingly appearing out of nowhere, but no one had been watching that direction. He was covered in camouflage including a camo mask that covered his face except for his mouth, nose and eyes.

"Just wanted to thank you for your work," BRH said in English. Heart translated for the Cantu. "I know you probably don't approve of all my methods, but we are on the same team. We all want to stop the poachers and others who would harm you."

Joseph asked why he was so secretive and a loner.

BRH responded that he must keep his identity a secret or the poachers would hurt him and his family.

"I'm only a loner when I'm doing my work. I have a family and a way of life that I get back to when I can. After the last couple weeks, I think it's time for a timeout. I just ask that you think of me in a good way." With that he disappeared back into the forest so quickly that it was almost like a dream.

Everyone in the entourage was looking at each other in disbelief.

After a minute or two, Joseph made sure everyone had their packs on correctly, then they started to walk. Knowing they were closer to getting back home, they walked with a bounce in their step.

Within an hour, the entourage returned with the prisoner in tow. The soldiers took him off to an enclosure where they would prepare to send him to jail. The soldiers and teens all began to clap as the jeeps pulled up. Abu told them the trip back would take just about half an hour.

The teens practically jumped into the jeeps. The Wantu and Cantu were more methodical. They knew from experience to move at a measured pace, to leave time to watch for any kind of sudden shift, or anything unsafe.

Kyle thought about his race car and joked that they could go faster.

Joseph spoke with Abu about returning the Cantu to their village; but first the tiny tribesmen were invited by the Wantu to join them for a community dinner.

The Cantu chief was quick to accept. After all, to decline such an invitation would be rude — besides, they were hungry.

***

When the entourage arrived at the Wantu camp, there were lots of group hugs and applause. The men, women and children in the camp came running to greet them and help unload their gear.

All were simply happy to see each other alive. The aroma from cooking embraced the travelers; the celebratory meal was already under way.

The homecoming hugs extended all around, to Sky and the visitors and even to the Cantu. All were treated as part of the family. Significantly, too, all had joined their Wantu brothers and sisters in their elemental fight.

The community feeling was of giddiness and joy as they shared their various stories. Tales were told about what happened from the time they left camp, and about their latest battle against the poachers and fire.

They were tearful too — both the Wantu and the visitors — knowing they would leave the next morning.

Joseph spoke quietly with Walden for a few minutes, then called the teens together in a group.

Sky, though not scheduled to leave the next day, was there to listen as well. He looked out at the horizon, musing. Then he looked at Joseph, the Wantu and the visitors.

"I need more time to reflect on everything that's happened since I fell from the sky," Sky began. "A few more months here, to gather my thoughts; but then I'll have to return home to my people. I need to remember my tribe and their ways. I have to remember who I am and what I believe."

"Take as much time as you need," said Joseph. "We consider you family. And that goes as well for all of you here."

"I thank you for your kindness, and your thoughts will be with me wherever I go," Sky replied.

"That goes for the rest of us too," Janet said. The others nodded.

Joseph asked the visitors what they had learned and how they would use it on their return.

Before they gave their answers individually, Massimo said he could speak briefly for the group, as the teens had discussed this walking back from the fire.

They'd come to love the Wantu and Cantu, this beautiful land and wildlife, he said. They'd come to love the peaceful tribal ways and culture, so they wanted to return as soon as they could, but it would most likely take a few years.

Massimo asked how he could get the money to him after the emeralds were sold. Joseph explained that the tribe had a bank

account, for both nonprofit donations and money needed for sup-
plies. The funds could be drawn on as needed, at the supply store. "It will be done," Massimo responded.

"I have every faith in you," Joseph returned with his smile.

"As for me," Massimo said, "I will work with my father on his trips for jewels. That way I'll find my way back here — but I am about so much more than the jewels. I will be involved with the International Wildlife Association to continue the battle against poaching, most especially the rhinos and the elephants."

"What he said," Janet added with love.

Cynthia said how impressed she was that the Wantu had no violence between couples. She planned to get involved with do-mestic violence-prevention groups, to see how she might help to reduce that problem.

Lizzy said she planned to work on Seattle environmental is-sues with Ben.

Kyle and PoRue said they would work together on the myriad environmental issues facing the Navajo Nation, from cleaning up uranium mines to recycling and addressing global-warming issues.

Then PoRue had the biggest surprise of all. "I'm going to con-tinue to work on various environmental causes, but my number-one priority is working to save endangered bats!"

Massimo gasped. "But that means you'll have to work in caves!"

"Exactly." She traded a look with Joseph. "A wish. To overcome my fears."

Author's Note

A mammal larger than most cars can be intimidating. The white rhino stands about seven feet tall. Think of a basketball player the width of a car and you understand that this is not a creature you want charging at you. The white rhino can also weigh up to 8,000 pounds. Imagine the impact of bing hit by that much weight.

While the white rhino has only one horn, it also has two horn-like growths on its snout, making it appear even more intimidating.

Nothing in the family Rhinocerotidae is small, but the white rhino is largest of all. Size is not everything, however; the white rhino is the most social of all rhinoceroses with both fellow rhinos and humans. While rhinos in the wild tend not to approach people, they are less likely to attack and more likely to get closer after they have seen us for a while.

The white rhino is sometimes white, but most are black or grey. It may not have been born that way, as much of its color comes from soil or bird droppings. Some believe it gets its color from the whiteness of its horn.

The white rhino is also a beast of beauty. It's so large and its skin is so thick; yet for those lucky enough to be able to touch one, the white rhino's skin is smooth.

Some might think that such a huge animal would be a meat-eater, but the white rhino lives wholly off grasses, vegetation and water, and can go five days without eating. Just as the white rhino doesn't eat anything except grass, leaves and berries, nature returns the favor, as it has no predators except poachers. Left to themselves, white rhinos can live up to 50 years.

For more information about the conservation of rhinos, elephants and other wildlife, go to the Lawrence Anthony Earth Organization.[1]

Suggested readings include Lawrence Anthony with Graham Spence, *The Last Rhinos: My Battle to Save One of the World's Greatest Creatures* (Thomas Dunne Books, 2012); ibid., *The Elephant Whisperer: My Life with the Herd in the African Wild* (Thomas Dunne Books, 2009); and Françoise Malby-Anthony with Katja Willemsen, *An Elephant in My Kitchen: What the Herd Taught Me About Love, Courage and Survival* (Thomas Dunne Books, 2019).

---

[1] (Earth Organization)

About the Author

Stan Bindell is a seasoned journalist with over 20 years in the field, having worked with the *Newark Star-Ledger* and as editor of the *Navajo-Hopi Observer*. For 25 years he has dedicated himself to teaching journalism and media, while continuing freelance writing.

Bindell's journalism career is marked by his coverage of environmental issues, such as uranium mining on Navajo and Hopi lands, the San Francisco Peaks ski resort, and potential mining near the Grand Canyon. He shares his passion for Arizona's wilderness through his YouTube channel, *Preserving Arizona Wilderness*, showcasing the region's natural beauty and recreational opportunities.

At Hopi Jr/Sr High School Bindell's students garnered state and national journalism awards. He pioneered the *Hopi High Teen Show*, a unique live Native American talk show broadcast via KUYI Hopi Radio, reaching a broad audience. Bindell also taught video journalism at Mingus High School till 2019, receiving the esteemed Forest Martin Award for his contributions to journalism education.

Today Bindell writes for several publications, including *The Navajo-Hopi Observer*, Prescott's *The Daily Courier* and *Flagstaff Business News*. His diverse contributions include Nativeand environmental news, business stories, and a hiking column. He's also shared his love for blues music as a disc jockey on KUYI Hopi Radio.

www.ingramcontent.com/pod-product-compliance
Lightning Source LLC
Chambersburg PA
CBHW060249100726
47907CB00003B/819